Fifty Shades of
Deception

About the Author

Estelle Winters is a master storyteller known for weaving intricate tales of power, betrayal, and haunting suspense. With a background steeped in understanding the complexities of human behavior and resilience, Estelle's stories delve deep into the shadows of the human psyche, revealing the vulnerabilities that drive her unforgettable characters.

Inspired by her own journey of overcoming life's darkest challenges, Estelle's work merges psychological depth with gothic atmospheres, creating narratives that linger long after the final page. Her latest novel, *Fifty Shades of Deception*, is a chilling exploration of control, legacy, and the consequences of buried secrets.

When she's not crafting her next spellbinding novel, Estelle enjoys exploring historic estates, drawing inspiration from their eerie beauty, and indulging in classic literature that ignites her imagination.

Table of CONTENTS

Prologue

The Game Begins

The mansion stood at the edge of the cliffs, its imposing silhouette etched against the twilight sky. Its stone walls, weathered by centuries of storms and salt air, bore the scars of time, yet exuded an unyielding strength. The iron gates, adorned with intricate carvings, stood slightly ajar, as if beckoning unwelcome visitors. Below, the sea churned and roared, its restless waves battering the jagged rocks with a relentless fury.

For generations, the Glenoire mansion had loomed over the small coastal town, casting a long shadow both literal and metaphorical. To the townsfolk, it was more than just a house. It was a legend, a warning, a curse. Stories of its dark history were whispered around campfires and at dimly lit taverns—stories of betrayal, tragedy, and unexplainable horrors. It was said that no one who entered the mansion's halls left unchanged, and many who entered never left at all. Yet, despite its sinister reputation, the mansion endured. It watched, silent and waiting, as the decades turned into centuries. And now, its latest occupant had arrived—Anastacia Graves.

The Legacy of the Glenoire Family

The story of the Glenoire mansion began in the mid-1800s, when Leopold Glenoire commissioned its construction. A man of immense wealth and ambition, Leopold had risen from humble beginnings to become one of the most powerful figures in the region. His investments in shipping, mining, and railroads had earned him a fortune, but his true obsession lay in the esoteric. While traveling through Europe, he had immersed himself in secret societies and forbidden knowledge, collecting artifacts and tomes said to hold the keys to power beyond mortal comprehension.

When Leopold returned to his homeland, he brought with him a vision—a mansion that would not only reflect his wealth but also serve as a nexus of arcane energy. The mansion was designed with meticulous care, its architecture blending Gothic and Victorian influences. Its sprawling halls and grand ballrooms were adorned with symbols and carvings whose meanings were known only to Leopold. Hidden rooms and secret passages were incorporated into the design, ensuring that the mansion held as many mysteries as its master.

Leopold's wife, Eliza, a striking and enigmatic woman, was said to be his partner in both business and occult endeavors.

Together, they hosted lavish parties that drew the elite from far and wide. But even amidst the opulence, whispers of strange rituals and sacrifices began to circulate. Servants claimed to hear chanting late at night, and some swore they saw shadows moving where no one stood.

Tragedy struck the Glenoire family early and often. Leopold's eldest son, Reginald, drowned under mysterious circumstances. His youngest, Victor, vanished one stormy night, leaving behind only his horse, found wandering the cliffs. Eliza, consumed by grief, withdrew from society and was found dead in her chambers years later. By the time Leopold himself succumbed to a sudden illness, the Glenoire legacy was one of sorrow and speculation.

The mansion changed hands several times after Leopold's death, but no one stayed for long. Strange accidents, unexplained phenomena, and a suffocating sense of dread drove each new owner away. The mansion's reputation grew darker with each passing year, until it was finally abandoned. For decades, it stood empty, its windows dark and its gates rusting, a monument to the Glenoires' cursed lineage.

The Townspeople's Stories

For years, the mansion sat in silence, its grand halls gathering dust, its gardens falling into ruin. But the town could never forget. The Glenoire mansion was a constant presence, a reminder of the family's dark history and the strange events that had taken place within its walls. The stories never stopped. Even as the Glenoire's became a distant memory, the mansion refused to fade from the townspeople's minds.

There were stories—some whispered, some told around campfires—about the mansion's influence on those who ventured too close. One old man, Jonas Tuck, claimed that when he was a boy, he and some friends had dared each other to sneak onto the grounds late at night. They had crept up to the mansion, the moonlight casting long shadows across the overgrown garden. Jonas swore that as they approached the front door, the windows had lit up with a pale, ghostly light, though no one had lived in the mansion for years. The boys had run, terrified, but Jonas had looked back, and what he saw chilled him to his bones. A woman stood in the window, watching them—her face pale, her eyes dark. He never went back.

Another story came from Mary Keaton, a local seamstress, who had been hired decades ago to help clean the mansion when it was briefly put up for sale. She had been in the library, dusting the shelves, when she felt a cold draft sweep through the room. The windows were shut, the doors closed, but the air had grown icy. When she turned around, she found the books on the shelves rearranged—letters spelled out on the spines, forming the word LIAR. Mary fled and never returned.

Over the years, many had tried to buy the mansion, drawn by its grandeur, its history, but none stayed for long. They would leave in the dead of night, pale and shaken, unwilling to speak of what had driven them away.

The mansion had a reputation, and it was well earned.

Then came Anastacia Graves.

She arrived without warning, a distant relative of the Glenoire's, though the exact connection was never clear. Some said she was the illegitimate child of one of the Glenoire men, others claimed she was the descendant of a distant cousin who had long since fled the cursed family. Whatever the truth, she had a claim to the estate, and she wasn't afraid to take it.

Anastacia Graves was not like the others who had come to the mansion before her. She was not driven by curiosity or greed, nor did she dismiss the stories as mere folklore. She came because the mansion was hers. A distant relative of the Glenoires, Anastacia had inherited the estate through a convoluted series of wills and family ties. To her, the mansion was an opportunity—a chance to start anew, to rebuild her life on her own terms.

From the moment she arrived, Anastacia made her presence known. She dismissed the whispers and warnings with a sharp laugh and a wave of her hand. The mansion, she claimed, was just a house, and she was its master. She set about restoring it with ruthless efficiency, hiring workers to repair the crumbling walls and overgrown gardens. The townsfolk watched from a distance, marveling at her confidence but muttering among themselves that she wouldn't last.

Anastacia's past was a mystery to most. She had spent her life climbing the ladder of success, using her wit, charm, and cunning to outmaneuver her rivals. But beneath her polished exterior was a woman who had been shaped by hardship. Her childhood had been one of neglect and manipulation, her parents teaching her that vulnerability was weakness and control was everything. She had learned to hide her emotions, to keep her true self locked away, and to wield power like a weapon.

The mansion, with its dark history and secrets, seemed a fitting home for someone like Anastacia. She thrived within its walls, turning it into both a fortress and a stage. But the mansion had its own plans. It watched her with unseen eyes, its presence growing stronger with each passing day. Anastacia believed she could bend the house to her will, but the house had been waiting for her. And it was patient.

Anastacia's Early Life: The Birth of a Survivor

To understand how Anastacia came to be the woman she was, you had to go back to her childhood. Born into a family that valued wealth and status above all else, Anastacia had learned early on that the world was a game, and only the ruthless survived. Her parents, distant and cold, had raised her to believe that emotions were a weakness. She was taught to manipulate, to calculate, to never let anyone see her true self.

Her father, a shrewd businessman, had been her first teacher. From the time she could walk, he would sit her down at the dining room table and quiz her on strategy, forcing her to think ten steps ahead. "The world is a chessboard," he would say, his voice devoid of affection. "If you're not the one making the moves, then you're the one being moved."

Her mother, a socialite with a penchant for cruelty, reinforced this lesson in her own way. She had taught Anastacia that appearances were everything, that what people saw mattered far more than what was real. "Let them believe what they want," her mother would say, brushing her hair in front of the grand mirror that dominated the living room. "As long as you're the one controlling the narrative." Anastacia had taken these lessons to heart. By the time she was a teenager, she had perfected the art of manipulation, bending others to her will with a smile or a whispered word. She was beautiful, smart, and utterly unafraid to use both to get what she wanted.

But even as she climbed the social and business ladders, there was always something inside her—a darkness that she couldn't quite explain. It was as though she had been born with a hollow space inside her, a space that no amount of success or wealth could fill. She learned to ignore it, to bury it deep within, but it was always there, waiting for the right moment to resurface.

When she inherited the mansion, she thought it would be the final piece of the puzzle, the thing that would finally give her the sense of power and control she craved. But the mansion had its own plans.

The mansion was a masterpiece of Gothic architecture, designed to impress and intimidate in equal measure. Its facade was built from dark stone, weathered by years of exposure to the sea's salt and the winds that howled relentlessly against the cliffs. The windows, tall and narrow, were framed in wrought iron, their glass panes thick and distorted, casting strange, rippling reflections within the house.

Inside, the mansion was a maze of long corridors, grand ballrooms, and dark, hidden corners. The floors were made of polished black marble, cold underfoot, and the walls were lined with portraits of the Glenoire family—stern-faced men and women who seemed to follow you with their eyes as you passed. The ceilings soared high above, adorned with intricate carvings and massive chandeliers that hung like spiders, their crystal teardrops casting fractured light across the rooms.

Every room had its own personality, its own history. The library, one of the largest rooms in the mansion, was filled with dusty, ancient books, many of which contained knowledge long forgotten by the outside world. The dining hall, with its massive oak table, had hosted countless feasts and gatherings, but now it sat empty, its chairs pushed back as though waiting for the next meal that would never come.

The bedrooms were equally grand, though they, too, had an air of decay. The beds were large and ornate, with canopies of heavy velvet that had long since faded to a dull, muted color. The fireplaces in each room were large enough to walk into, their grates cold and unused. But it was the mirrors that drew the most attention. There were mirrors in almost every room, some as tall as the walls themselves, others small and round, but all of them seemed to hold a presence, as though they were windows to something far older and darker than the world outside.

And then there was the ballroom—the heart of the mansion. It was vast, its floor made of polished marble that gleamed in the flickering light of the chandeliers above. The walls were lined with tall mirrors, and in the center of the room was a grand staircase that led to the upper floors. It was in this ballroom that the most notorious events of the mansion's history had taken place—grand parties that ended in tragedy, whispered conversations that led to betrayal, and, most recently, Anastacia's masquerade ball, where the game had begun.

The mansion had always been a place of secrets, but now it was something more. It was alive, and it was watching.

The Storm Approaches: The Game Begins

Now, as the storm gathered on the horizon, the mansion stirred. The air grew heavy, thick with the scent of rain and salt. The wind picked up, whistling through the cracks in the stone and rattling the shutters. Inside, the shadows deepened, stretching across the floors like fingers reaching for something unseen.

Anastacia stood in the grand study, gazing out at the churning sea. The manuscript lay open on the desk before her, its pages filled with her careful, deliberate handwriting. She had been working on it for weeks, pouring her thoughts and memories into the story, shaping it with the same precision she applied to every aspect of her life. But now, as she stared at the final lines, an unease she couldn't name began to creep over her.

"This is your story," the voice whispered, soft and cold. "But you are not the author."

She turned sharply, her eyes scanning the empty room. The house was quiet, but she could feel it—the weight of its presence, the sense that she was being watched. She shook her head, dismissing the thought, and returned to her desk. But the feeling lingered, growing stronger with each passing moment.

Outside, the storm broke, the first drops of rain splattering against the windows. The wind howled, and the mansion groaned in response, as though waking from a long slumber. Anastacia's grip tightened on her pen as she forced herself to focus on the manuscript. She would finish this. She had to.

But deep down, she knew the truth. The mansion was alive, and it was waiting. The game was about to begin.

Part I:

Whispers in the Shadows

Chapter 1

Whispers from the Deep

The sea churned violently beneath the cliffs, its waves crashing with a thunderous roar that reverberated up the jagged rocks and into the stillness of the mansion. Anastacia stood at the edge of the balcony, her hands gripping the cold iron railing, her eyes fixed on the horizon where storm clouds gathered like a funeral shroud. The wind whipped her hair around her face, the salt-laden air stinging her skin. The storm was coming—both outside and within her.

She exhaled slowly, yet the tension in her shoulders refused to release, despite the vastness of the view in front of her. For years, this balcony had been her sanctuary, a place to think, to plan, to manipulate. From here, she could see the expanse of the ocean, the jagged cliffs, and the narrow path that led up to the mansion—a fortress perched high above the tumultuous sea. It was a place of power, and she had always felt in control here. But lately, something had shifted. The wind carried a faint whisper, barely audible, but enough to make her turn sharply, her eyes scanning the empty terrace behind her. No one was there, yet the feeling lingered—that sense of being watched, of being judged. It had been growing stronger over the past few weeks, a creeping sensation that settled into her bones, making her question everything around her. The mansion had always felt alive in its own way, its creaking floors and shifting shadows part of its charm, but now it seemed more… conscious. As though it had woken up and was watching her every move.

She turned her back on the ocean and walked inside, pulling the balcony doors shut behind her. The wind howled in protest, rattling the glass panes as if it, too, wanted to enter. Anastacia needed the quiet, the stillness, to gather her thoughts. Her 50th birthday was approaching, and with it came a sense of dread she couldn't quite place. Birthdays had never bothered her before—she had always seen age as a marker of her accomplishments, another year of outmaneuvering her enemies, of building her empire. But this year felt different. This year, the shadows seemed longer, the nights darker.

As she moved through the grand sitting room, her heels clicked softly against the polished wood floors. The room was bathed in the golden light of the setting sun, the massive windows overlooking the sea casting long shadows across the room. She paused in front of the grand mirror that dominated one wall, her reflection staring back at her—

serene, poised, and as controlled as ever. But even here, in the safety of her own home, there was something unsettling about her reflection. It wasn't quite right, as though the person staring back at her was wearing a mask—her face, but not her soul.

She tilted her head, watching her reflection as if it would reveal some hidden truth about the unease that had been growing within her. It wasn't the approaching birthday alone that made her feel this way. It was the sensation that things were slipping out of her grasp, that no matter how tightly she held on, the world she had built was beginning to unravel. For years, she had carefully curated every detail of her life—both personal and professional. Her rise to power had been deliberate, calculated. She had sacrificed, betrayed, and manipulated to reach the top, and now she felt the weight of those choices bearing down on her.

Anastacia's mind flickered back to the early years, when everything had been simpler but the stakes had still been high. Her family's business empire had been vast, sprawling across multiple industries. Her father, a man of immense influence and a ruthlessness she had inherited, had always told her that control was everything. She remembered those words as if they had been etched into her very being. Control was power, and power was survival.

She had been just twenty-five when she took her place in the boardroom for the first time. It was a pivotal moment, one that she had been groomed for her entire life. The room had been filled with men—all older, all dismissive of her presence. They had seen her as nothing more than a figurehead, a young woman to be manipulated, underestimated. But Anastacia had learned early on how to wield the very thing they underestimated—her gender, her youth—as a weapon.

Her father had been behind her in those days, guiding her through the political minefield of corporate power. But even as he taught her, Anastacia knew that his support was conditional. Her value was measured by her ability to maintain control. She had watched him use people like pawns, discarding them the moment they no longer served his purposes, and she had vowed never to become one of those pawns. She had become the player instead.

In that first boardroom meeting, she had said little, listening more than speaking, learning the weaknesses of those around her. But by the end of the meeting, she had made her presence known. One of the senior executives had tried to undermine her, suggesting that she lacked the experience to contribute meaningfully to the conversation. She had smiled—a smile that had become her signature—and then, with a single, cutting remark, she had dismantled his argument, turning the tables on him so swiftly that by the time he realized what had happened, it was too late. He was outmaneuvered.

From that moment on, Anastacia had never looked back. Each victory, each conquest, had added another layer to the fortress she had built around herself. Emotions were weaknesses, and weaknesses were something she had long since learned to bury.

A knock on the door broke the silence, drawing Anastacia out of her thoughts. She turned to see Nathaniel standing in the doorway, his face as troubled as ever. He was her brother, the only other person who knew the true depths of the family's legacy, but their relationship had always been strained. Where Anastacia had thrived in the shadows of power and manipulation, Nathaniel had struggled, weighed down by his insecurities and fears. He had always been the anxious one, the one who saw shadows where there were none. And lately, his anxiety had taken on a darker edge, one that Anastacia found increasingly difficult to tolerate.

"Nathaniel," she said coolly, her voice cutting through the tension that hung between them. "What is it now? More of your cryptic warnings?"

He stepped into the room, hesitating for a moment before speaking. "Anastacia, we need to talk."

She sighed, running a hand through her hair, already weary of whatever drama he was about to unleash. "What is it this time?"

"It's not just me," Nathaniel said, his voice strained. His eyes darted to the mirror before returning to her. "The mansion... it's changing. You feel it, don't you?"

She scoffed, though his words hit closer to home than she cared to admit. "Nathaniel, the mansion is old. It creaks. It groans. It makes strange noises in the night. That's what old houses do."

"No, this is different," Nathaniel insisted, stepping closer. "The air feels heavier. The shadows... they're darker, deeper. And I've been having dreams. Dreams about the past, about things we've never spoken about."

A chill ran down Anastacia's spine, but she kept her expression neutral, refusing to let him see the effect his words were having on her. She had always prided herself on her ability to control her emotions, to keep her fears buried deep where no one could see them. "Nathaniel, you're letting your imagination run wild. This house has stood for over a hundred years. It's seen more storms, more tragedies, and more secrets than you or I will ever know. But it's just a house."

Nathaniel shook his head, his frustration mounting. "Anastacia, please. I think something is waking up. Something tied to our family's past. The dreams... they're warnings."

She turned away from him, walking toward the window. The sky was darkening, the storm drawing closer, the clouds swirling ominously above the sea. "You and your superstitions," she muttered. "I don't have time for this."

But before she could dismiss him entirely, Nathaniel grabbed her arm, his grip tighter than she expected. She turned to face him, her eyes narrowing in anger. "You have to listen to me," he said, his voice trembling. "The past is coming back. And if we don't do something about it, it will consume us."

Anastacia yanked her arm free, her temper flaring. "Enough, Nathaniel! I don't want to hear any more about your dreams or your fears. This is my house, my life, and I am in control of it. Not you, not the past, and certainly not some ridiculous curse you've conjured up in your head."

Nathaniel's face fell, the weight of his words sinking into the silence between them. He took a step back, his shoulders slumping in defeat. "You'll see," he whispered, his voice barely audible. "You'll see soon enough."

With that, he turned and left the room, his footsteps echoing through the empty hall, leaving Anastacia alone with the storm outside and the growing unease inside her chest.

For a long time, she stood there, staring out at the sea, her reflection faint in the glass. But no matter how hard she tried to shake off Nathaniel's words, they clung to her, like the dampness in the air, refusing to let go.

The Mansion's Eerie Presence

As the evening deepened and the storm outside reached its full fury, Anastacia retreated deeper into the mansion. The wind howled, rattling the windows, and the floorboards creaked beneath her feet, as if the house were shifting, settling into itself. The mansion had always been imposing, but tonight, it felt different. The walls seemed to breathe, the shadows clinging more tightly to the corners of every room. She wandered aimlessly, her mind caught between Nathaniel's warnings and her own mounting anxieties. Her 50th birthday was only days away, and with it came the weight of everything she had achieved—and everything she had lost. The empire she had built was solid, unshakable, but it had cost her dearly. She had sacrificed relationships, her own emotional well-being, and any semblance of vulnerability in exchange for power.

The strange occurrences around the mansion seemed to mirror the turmoil inside her. Objects weren't where she had left them. A vase in the hallway appeared on the dining room table, the scent of flowers fresh even though they were days old. Lights flickered in the grand sitting room, and once, she thought she saw a figure in the hallway—a shadow moving just beyond the reach of the lamplight. But when she blinked, it was gone.

She paused in the grand staircase, her hand resting on the smooth, cool railing, and looked up at the massive chandelier hanging above. Its crystals swayed gently, though there was no draft in the room. It cast distorted reflections on the walls, the light bending and twisting as if the mansion itself was playing tricks on her.

Anastacia closed her eyes, leaning against the banister as memories of her younger self flooded her mind. There had been a time when she wasn't so hard, when the ambition hadn't yet hardened her heart to the point of no return. She had loved once, truly loved, but that had been her downfall. His name had been Michael. They had met when she was in her early thirties, just as her rise in the family business was reaching its peak. He had been everything she hadn't known she needed—kind, steady, with none of the sharp edges she possessed. For a while, she had let herself believe that she could have both: love and power, vulnerability and control. But the deeper she fell for him, the more she realized that one would have to give way for the other.

Michael had wanted her to soften, to let go of the relentless drive that consumed her. He had asked her once, in a moment of quiet intimacy, why she needed to control everything. She had brushed off the question, but it had lingered, gnawing at the edges of her mind. He had seen through her, seen the part of her that still longed for something more than power.

But in the end, she had chosen her path. She had let Michael slip away, pushing him out of her life because she couldn't afford the weakness his love represented. And in doing so, she had sealed her fate. There would be no more softness, no more vulnerability. She had hardened herself, closed off the parts of her that might have allowed her to be anything other than the cold, calculating woman she had become.

The memories faded, leaving Anastacia feeling raw, exposed in a way she hadn't felt in years. She opened her eyes and straightened, pushing the past away once more. There was no room for regret, not now. She had chosen her path, and she would walk it to the end, no matter where it led.

But as she ascended the stairs, her footsteps echoing in the vast silence of the mansion, she couldn't shake the feeling that the past wasn't done with her yet. Nathaniel's words echoed in her mind, mingling with the growing sense of dread that had settled over her like a shroud.

The past is coming back.

And no matter how hard she tried to outrun it, it was catching up to her.

Chapter 2

Beneath the Tempest

The rain fell in thick sheets, drumming against the windows of the mansion with a relentless rhythm that matched the pounding in Anastacia's head. She sat at her desk in the study, staring at the folder in front of her—the one that held all the answers she had been dreading for weeks. Inside were the results of the investigation she had ordered into Daniel, her husband, and the truth about his late nights, suspicious phone calls, and sudden distance.

Her hand hovered over the folder, her fingers trembling ever so slightly. She wasn't sure why she hadn't opened it yet. Perhaps because once she did, there would be no going back. The truth would be out, and the carefully constructed façade of her marriage would shatter like glass. But wasn't that what she wanted—the truth? Wasn't it?

The storm outside howled louder, as if nature itself was warning her not to proceed, but Anastacia had never been one to back down from confrontation, especially when betrayal was involved. With a sharp breath, she flipped the folder open, scanning its contents in a blur of anger and disbelief. The photos, reports, and phone records were all there, laid out in excruciating detail, each one hammering home the betrayal.

Daniel was having an affair.

Not just any affair—with Alexandra, her former best friend. The rage that welled up inside Anastacia was so fierce, so all-consuming, that for a moment, she thought she might actually be sick. Her fingers gripped the sides of the folder, knuckles white as she struggled to maintain control. How could Daniel do this to her? How could Alexandra? The betrayal from her closest confidante cut even deeper than Daniel's infidelity. Alexandra had been like a sister to her, had known her secrets, had stood by her through countless storms—only to become the storm herself.

Anastacia's vision blurred with fury, her breath coming in shallow, ragged gasps. She slammed the folder shut, the impact reverberating through the quiet study. Pain and anger clawed at her insides, each thought of their deceit twisting the knife deeper.

But beneath the rage was something else—something colder, more calculated. She could feel it rising from the pit of her stomach like a slow, simmering poison.

Revenge.

They would pay for this. Both of them.

But not in a fit of rage. No, Anastacia wasn't reckless; she was meticulous. She wouldn't lash out without a plan. She would destroy them both, piece by piece, until they were left with nothing. But it would be done carefully, methodically, in a way that left no trace back to her.

Her thoughts raced, calculating the steps ahead. Daniel had made the first move, but she would have the last. The storm outside intensified, the wind howling in time with her heartbeat. She stood abruptly, pushing the chair back with such force that it toppled over. The walls seemed to close in on her, the shadows deepening, as if the mansion itself was feeding off her turmoil.

I need to move. She stormed out of the study, her footsteps echoing through the empty halls of the mansion. The wind rattled the windows, the storm outside raging in sync with the one inside her. As she reached the grand staircase, she gripped the banister tightly, staring down at the empty entryway.

The rage and betrayal coursing through her veins were too powerful to contain, too visceral to ignore. She wanted to destroy something, to feel the power of control again, to take action. And then, suddenly, she stopped. Control. That was the key. She would not allow herself to be a victim. She would not allow anyone to take control of her life.

The shadows in the hall seemed to shift and pulse, as though the mansion itself was aware of her plan. It had always been a place of power for her, a sanctuary where she could retreat and rebuild. But now it felt like something more—a fortress readying itself for war.

As she turned, ready to return to the study, a figure appeared in the entryway.

Marcus.

His coat dripped with rain, his dark eyes intense as they locked onto hers. For a moment, the world outside seemed to still, the storm quieting just enough for her to hear her own heartbeat. She hadn't seen Marcus in years—not since… No. She wouldn't think about that now.

"Marcus," Anastacia said, her voice steady despite the tumult inside her. "What are you doing here?"

He didn't answer immediately. Instead, he took a step forward, the weight of his presence filling the room. His movements were slow, deliberate, as if he knew the impact he had on her. "I heard about the party you're planning," he said finally, his voice low and rough. "I thought I'd stop by early."

Anastacia frowned, crossing her arms over her chest defensively. "You're early, all right. The party isn't for another two months."

He shrugged, his eyes never leaving hers. "Maybe I just wanted to see you."

The tension between them was thick, palpable, a lingering echo of the past they had tried to bury. But the past had a way of resurfacing, no matter how deep you tried to push it down. Anastacia felt the familiar pull of Marcus, the way he could get under her skin, make her feel things she had long since buried.

She clenched her jaw, her fingers digging into her arms. "We don't have anything to say to each other, Marcus. Not anymore."

He took another step forward, closing the distance between them. "You sure about that?"

Her breath caught in her throat, her pulse quickening. She had always hated the way he could make her feel so out of control, so vulnerable. But she refused to let him see it.

"Yes," she said coldly, turning her back on him and walking toward the parlor. "I'm sure."

But as she walked away, she could feel his eyes on her, burning into her back, and she knew—no matter how hard she tried to ignore it—that the past was far from over.

While the storm outside raged, Alexandra's betrayal replayed itself over and over in Anastacia's mind. How had she not seen it? How had she been so blind? Alexandra had always been close to her, too close perhaps. She had trusted her implicitly, sharing confidences, building a friendship that had seemed unbreakable. But Alexandra had betrayed her—had stolen not just her husband, but her trust. Anastacia couldn't help but wonder how it had started. Was it planned? Was Alexandra always lurking, waiting to strike when Anastacia was at her weakest?

Alexandra had come into Anastacia's life unexpectedly. They had met at an elite business conference years ago, drawn together by their shared ambition and drive. Alexandra was brilliant, charismatic, and quick-witted, with a keen eye for detail that had immediately impressed Anastacia. The two had become fast friends, and soon, Alexandra had become a fixture in Anastacia's life—her closest confidante, her trusted ally.

But Alexandra had always been more than what she appeared. Beneath the polished exterior and easy charm, there was a hunger—a need to prove herself, to rise above the constraints of her background. Alexandra had grown up with nothing, clawing her way to the top through sheer determination and grit. And while Anastacia admired that about her, she now realized that it was also what made Alexandra dangerous.

In hindsight, the signs had been there. Alexandra's subtle flirtations with Daniel, the way she had always seemed just a little too interested in his affairs. But Anastacia had ignored them, too consumed by her own power plays to see the truth. And Daniel—how long had he been a willing participant in this betrayal? Had their marriage always been a charade, or had he genuinely loved her once? Anastacia felt the sting of his deception like a physical blow, but she refused to show weakness. If anything, it only fueled her resolve.

They both thought they could get away with this. But they didn't know who they were dealing with.

By the time she reached the study again, Anastacia's mind was already in motion, plotting her next move. Alexandra and Daniel might think they had the upper hand, but they were playing in her world. Anastacia had built her empire on the ruins of those who had crossed her. She knew how to destroy someone completely, to erase their influence and leave them begging for scraps.

But this had to be done right. If she moved too quickly, it would look like a petty revenge. Anastacia wasn't interested in petty. She wanted total annihilation—both personally and professionally.

She needed allies. People who could help her execute her plan without raising suspicion.

Anastacia's business network was vast, but there were a few key people she trusted implicitly. One of them was Caroline, her personal assistant. Caroline had been with Anastacia for nearly a decade, a sharp, no-nonsense woman who had proven her loyalty time and time again. If anyone could help Anastacia navigate the delicate web of revenge she was weaving, it was Caroline.

Anastacia picked up the phone, dialing Caroline's number.

"Ms. Graves?" Caroline's voice came through the receiver, crisp and professional, as always.

"I need you to come to the mansion," Anastacia said, her tone leaving no room for argument. "There's something I need your help with."

"I'll be there in an hour."

Anastacia hung up the phone, feeling a sense of satisfaction. Caroline would handle the logistics. But she needed more than just strategy. She needed someone with influence in the financial world—someone who could quietly destabilize Daniel's assets without it tracing back to her.

That's where Henry came in.

Henry was an investment advisor who had been instrumental in several of Anastacia's more… discreet business dealings. He had a reputation for being ruthless, and Anastacia knew he wouldn't hesitate to get his hands dirty if the price was right.

As Anastacia waited for Caroline and Henry to arrive, the storm outside intensified, the wind battering the windows with a ferocity that mirrored her inner turmoil. She stood by the window, watching the rain fall in heavy sheets, obscuring the view of the sea below. Lightning flashed in the distance, illuminating the jagged cliffs for a brief moment before plunging them back into darkness.

The storm wasn't just outside—it was inside her, too. A swirling, chaotic force that threatened to tear her apart if she didn't control it. But control was what Anastacia did best. She would harness this storm, bend it to her will, and use it to destroy the people who had betrayed her.

By the time Caroline and Henry arrived, Anastacia was calm, collected, and ready to begin her campaign of revenge.

Caroline entered the study first, her sharp eyes immediately taking in the tension in the room. "What's going on, Ms. Graves?"

Anastacia gestured to the folder on the desk. "Daniel is having an affair. With Alexandra."

Caroline's expression didn't falter. She had been by Anastacia's side long enough to know that this wasn't the time for shock or pity. "What do you want me to do?"

"I want you to start digging into Alexandra's background. Find anything we can use to ruin her. Financial records, personal scandals—whatever you can find. Quietly."

Caroline nodded, already making notes on her phone. "And Daniel?"

Anastacia's lips curled into a cold smile. "I'll handle Daniel myself."

Just then, Henry entered the room, his tall frame filling the doorway. He glanced between Anastacia and Caroline, sensing the seriousness of the situation. "You called?"

Anastacia nodded. "I need you to start moving Daniel's investments. Slowly. Quietly. Make it look like market forces are working against him. I want him to feel the pressure, but I don't want him to know where it's coming from."

Henry arched an eyebrow, but didn't question her. "Consider it done."

With her team in place, Anastacia felt the first stirrings of satisfaction. This was what she did best—pulling the strings, controlling the narrative, bending people to her will.

The storm raged on outside, but inside, Anastacia was finally beginning to feel like herself again.

As the days passed, Anastacia's plan began to unfold exactly as she had envisioned. Alexandra's carefully constructed image began to crack as Caroline uncovered a series of scandals from her past—misappropriated funds, questionable dealings, rumors of affairs with other high-profile men. One by one, Anastacia leaked the information to the right people, ensuring that Alexandra's reputation would be irreparably damaged.

Meanwhile, Daniel's financial situation took a sudden downturn. Henry had worked his magic, subtly shifting Daniel's investments until they began to hemorrhage money. At first, Daniel didn't notice, too consumed by his affair and his growing distance from Anastacia. But soon, the financial losses became too large to ignore. He tried to fix things, but it was too late. The damage had been done.

And through it all, Anastacia remained calm, serene even, as she watched the pieces of her revenge fall into place.

But there was still one final act to play.

The storm outside had reached its peak, the wind howling so fiercely that it rattled the very foundation of the mansion. Anastacia stood in the parlor, waiting for Daniel to return from his latest trip. He was oblivious to what had been happening behind the scenes, to the fact that his world was about to come crashing down.

When he finally walked through the door, drenched from the rain, Anastacia felt a surge of satisfaction. This was it—the moment she had been waiting for.

"Anastacia," Daniel said, shaking the rain from his coat. "I didn't expect you to be up."

She smiled, a slow, deliberate smile that sent a chill down his spine. "We need to talk."

Daniel frowned, sensing that something was off. "What's this about?"

Anastacia didn't answer right away. Instead, she crossed the room, her heels clicking softly on the polished wood floor. She stopped in front of the fireplace, the flames casting flickering shadows on her face.

"It's about Alexandra," she said finally, her voice as cold as the storm outside.

Daniel froze, his eyes widening in shock. "What are you talking about?"

Anastacia turned to face him, her expression unreadable. "I know about the affair, Daniel. I know everything."

The color drained from his face, and for a moment, he looked like a man on the verge of collapse. But then, just as quickly, he recovered, straightening his shoulders and narrowing his eyes.

"How did you—"

"It doesn't matter how I found out," Anastacia interrupted. "What matters is that I did."

For a long moment, they stood there in silence, the only sound the crackling of the fire and the distant roar of the storm. Then, finally, Daniel spoke.

"What are you going to do?"

Anastacia smiled again, a cold, calculating smile that sent a shiver down his spine. "I've already done it."

As the storm outside reached its peak, Anastacia felt the full weight of her actions settling over her. She had won. She had destroyed Alexandra and Daniel, just as she had planned. But as she stood in the parlor, watching the rain pound against the windows, she couldn't shake the feeling that something was still missing.

The mansion seemed to groan under the weight of the storm, its old bones creaking and shifting. Anastacia felt a strange sense of unease, as though the house itself was reacting to the turmoil inside her. The shadows in the corners of the room seemed darker, deeper, as if they were watching her, waiting for her next move.

And as she stared into the fire, she realized that the storm inside her was far from over.

The past had a way of coming back, no matter how carefully you tried to bury it.

Chapter 3

The Shadow's Loom

The mansion had become a prison.

Every room, every hallway, felt like it was closing in around her, suffocating her with its heavy air and shifting shadows. Anastacia moved through the house like a ghost, her mind a whirlwind of plans and paranoia. The storm outside had finally passed, but the storm inside the mansion was just beginning.

The strange occurrences had started small. A cold draft in rooms that should have been warm. Doors that creaked open on their own. Mirrors that reflected things she couldn't explain. Then her dog, Max, had died.

She had found him lying at the foot of her bed one crisp morning, his body cold and stiff, his eyes wide and lifeless. The vet had said it was natural causes—old age. But Anastacia knew better. Max had been in perfect health the day before, bounding through the halls with his usual exuberance. The suddenness of his death gnawed at her.

But it wasn't just the loss of Max that unsettled her. It was the note she found tucked under her pillow that morning, as if someone or something had crept into her room while she slept. A single piece of paper, crumpled and worn, with one word scrawled in red ink:

Liar.

Her hands had trembled as she held the note, her mind racing with questions. Who had left it? What did it mean? And why did it feel like the mansion itself was watching her, waiting for her to make a mistake?

She had shown the note to Nathaniel, but his response had only deepened her anxiety. He had shrugged, his face pale and drawn, dark circles beneath his eyes. "I told you," he had whispered. "I told you something was happening in this house."

Anastacia wasn't ready to believe him, not yet. There had to be a logical explanation for everything. There had to be.

She paced the grand sitting room, her thoughts spiraling out of control. Max's death, the note, the eerie sensations that pervaded the mansion—it all pointed to something darker, something more insidious lurking beneath the surface. Marcus had been acting strange ever since he had arrived, watching her too closely, his eyes filled with something she couldn't name. And Nathaniel… he was unraveling right in front of her, his paranoia growing with each passing day. She had caught him more than once standing in front of the walls, running his fingers over the wallpaper, muttering under his breath about their family's past.

She didn't know who to trust anymore.

The mansion had a way of twisting the truth, bending reality until she couldn't tell where her mind ended and the house began.

Max had been her companion through everything, loyal and unwavering. His presence had grounded her, a constant in a life filled with shifting power dynamics and betrayals. Anastacia vividly remembered the day she brought Max to the mansion, a tiny puppy back then, scampering through the grand halls with boundless energy.

But over the past few weeks, Max had become restless, barking at empty corners, growling at doors that hadn't been opened. She had thought it was just age catching up with him, his senses dulling, his mind playing tricks. But now, standing in the shadowy light of the sitting room, she wasn't so sure. Max had always been sensitive to things beyond human perception. He had sensed something she hadn't.

The mansion had taken him.

And now, the same dark force that had claimed Max seemed to be working its way through her, manipulating her thoughts, feeding off her fears.

Anastacia and Marcus: Unresolved Tensions

The knock at the door pulled Anastacia from her thoughts. She turned sharply, her heart skipping a beat. Marcus was standing in the doorway, his coat still wet from the rain, his eyes dark and intense as they locked onto hers.

Their history together was tangled, complicated. They had known each other for years, but their relationship had always been strained, filled with unspoken tensions and unresolved feelings. Marcus had once been someone she trusted, someone she had relied on. But that trust had been broken a long time ago.

"Marcus," Anastacia said, her voice cool and steady despite the turmoil inside her. "What are you doing here?"

He stepped into the room, his presence filling the space like a shadow that refused to leave. He didn't answer immediately, instead taking his time to scan the room before turning his gaze back to her. "I heard about Max," he said finally, his voice low and rough.

Anastacia stiffened. "How did you hear about that?"

Marcus shrugged. "Word travels."

She crossed her arms, her eyes narrowing. "You still haven't answered my question. Why are you here?"

For a moment, Marcus said nothing, his gaze never leaving hers. Then, slowly, he took another step closer, closing the distance between them. "I wanted to see you. To talk. It's been a long time, Anastacia."

She felt a flicker of something—an old wound reopening. There had been a time when she and Marcus had been close, closer than she had ever been with anyone else. They had shared secrets, plans, dreams. But that was before… before everything had fallen apart.

"You shouldn't have come," she said, her voice sharp. "We have nothing to talk about."

"Don't we?" His tone was soft, yet it cut through the tension in the room like a knife. "What happened between us, Anastacia?"

Her pulse quickened. She had always hated the way Marcus could get under her skin, the way he could make her feel things she had long since buried. But she refused to let him see it. She had built her life on control, and Marcus represented everything she couldn't control.

"It's in the past," she said coldly, turning her back on him. "Let it stay there."

But as she walked away, she could feel his eyes on her, burning into her back. The past wasn't as distant as she wanted it to be, and no matter how hard she tried to ignore it, Marcus's presence stirred something inside her—something she had thought she had buried long ago.

Years ago, Anastacia and Marcus had been inseparable. They had built empires together, both in business and in their personal lives. There had been an intensity between them, a magnetic pull that neither of them could deny. But that intensity had turned toxic.

Marcus had betrayed her in a way that no one else could. It hadn't been business; it had been personal. He had gotten too close, too entangled in her emotions, and when she had let her guard down, he had used it against her. She had trusted him with her darkest secrets, and in the end, he had abandoned her when she needed him most.

It had been over a decade since they had parted ways, but the wound still ached. Every time she saw him, the pain resurfaced, a reminder of the one person who had truly known her and had still walked away.

Now, standing in the dim light of the sitting room, she couldn't shake the feeling that Marcus hadn't just come back to check on her. There was more to his visit—there always was.

"You're still angry," Marcus said, his voice breaking through her thoughts.

She turned to face him, her eyes hard. "I'm not angry. I'm indifferent."

He chuckled softly, but there was no humor in it. "You're never indifferent, Anastacia. That's not who you are."

She clenched her jaw, refusing to give him the satisfaction of a response. Marcus always had a way of seeing through her defenses, but this time, she wouldn't let him.

"What do you want, Marcus?" she asked, her voice cold.

He took a step closer, his eyes searching hers. "I want to help you."

Anastacia felt a flicker of suspicion. "Help me? With what?"

"With whatever's happening in this house," he said, his voice low and serious. "I can feel it, Anastacia. Something's wrong here. Something dark."

She narrowed her eyes, studying him carefully. For years, she had learned to read people, to see through their lies and their facades. But with Marcus, it was different. She could never quite tell what he was thinking.

"I don't need your help," she said firmly.

But even as she said the words, she wasn't sure she believed them.

Later that evening, Anastacia sat in her study, her mind racing with the events of the day. Max's death, Marcus's sudden appearance, the growing tension in the mansion—it was all building to something, something she couldn't quite grasp.

A knock on the door pulled her from her thoughts. Simon stood in the doorway, his expression tense. Simon was her publisher, her business partner, and someone she had once considered a friend. But lately, even Simon had been acting strangely.

"Anastacia," he said, stepping into the room, his voice quiet. "We need to talk."

She crossed her arms, her eyes narrowing. "About what?"

Simon hesitated, his gaze flickering toward the windows as though he was afraid of being overheard. "I've been getting letters."

Anastacia frowned. "Letters?"

He nodded, running a hand through his hair. "Threats. Someone wants your new book. They're demanding it be released… or else."

She stared at him, her mind racing. "What are you talking about? The book isn't even finished yet."

"I know," he said, his voice shaking slightly. "But they don't care. They're saying… they're saying if you don't release it, something bad will happen."

Anastacia's stomach twisted, the weight of his words settling over her like a heavy fog. "Who sent these letters?"

Simon shook his head, his eyes dark with fear. "I don't know. They were unsigned. But whoever it is… they know things,

Anastacia. Personal things. Things about you, about your life."

A chill ran down her spine. "What kind of things?"

He swallowed hard, his voice barely above a whisper. "Things from the book. Things you haven't even written yet."

The room seemed to tilt around her, her mind reeling with the implications of his words. How could they know? How could anyone know what she hadn't written?

Unless…

Unless someone was watching her. Someone who knew her better than she knew herself.

The note, the letters, the strange occurrences in the mansion—it all started to connect, the pieces of the puzzle falling into place. Someone was playing a game with her, manipulating her life, her thoughts, her work.

But who?

And why?

Her hands clenched into fists, her breath coming in short, sharp bursts. She had to find out. She had to take back control.

But as she stood there, staring at Simon, the room around her seemed to grow darker, the shadows creeping closer, the air thickening with a palpable tension. The mansion was watching, waiting.

And for the first time in her life, Anastacia felt truly afraid.

The strange occurrences around the mansion had been growing more frequent, more intense. At first, it had been subtle—small things out of place, a shadow that didn't quite belong, a cold draft where there shouldn't have been one. But now, it was undeniable. The house was alive. It was breathing, watching, waiting.

Late one night, as Anastacia walked through the darkened halls, she noticed something strange. Symbols, faint but unmistakable, had appeared on the walls—intricate patterns that seemed to pulse with a dark energy. She ran her fingers over them, feeling the rough texture of the stone beneath her fingertips. The symbols weren't part of the original design of the house. Someone had put them there, recently.

As she walked further down the hall, she heard a sound—faint at first, but growing louder. It was a whisper, just out of reach, as though someone—or something—was calling to her. She followed the sound, her heart racing, until she reached the grand staircase.

There, at the foot of the stairs, she saw it.

A shadow.

But it wasn't just a shadow. It was something more.

Something darker. It moved slowly, deliberately, as though

it was watching her, waiting for her to come closer.

Anastacia took a step back, her breath catching in her throat.

The mansion was no longer just a house. It was a living,

breathing entity. And it wanted something from her.

She turned and ran, her footsteps echoing through the empty

halls, the shadows following close behind.

Part II:

Masks and Mirrors

Chapter 4

Dark Revelations

The storm outside the mansion mirrored the storm brewing inside Anastacia's mind. The sky, a bruised purple, hung low over the sea, churning waves against the cliffs like a dark omen. Anastacia stood in her study, the faint glow of her computer screen casting a pallid light on her face. Her fingers hovered over the keyboard as she reread the email she had crafted for her party guests—a masterpiece of subtle malice. Each line was laced with enough ambiguity to plant seeds of doubt, suspicion, and fear. It was perfect.

She leaned back in her leather chair, the creak of it lost in the sound of the wind howling outside. The mansion groaned in response, its walls seeming to breathe with the tension that permeated the air. A shiver ran down her spine, though the room was warm. It wasn't the weather that unsettled her—it was the mansion. Lately, it felt as though it had come alive. Every shadow seemed deeper, every creak louder, every mirror reflecting something just slightly off. She had lived here for years, yet recently, it had begun to feel like an entirely different place. A sentient place.

She clicked "Send" on the email. A smile curled on her lips as she imagined the reactions of her guests. They would receive their invitations soon enough—an invitation to a party where their darkest secrets would be laid bare. Not overtly, of course. That wasn't her style. No, the game she had designed for her 50th birthday celebration would be elegant and subtle, a scavenger hunt with clues so well-hidden that only the truly paranoid would be able to piece them together. And once they did, it would be too late.

The first part of the game would take place during the party, with her guests unwittingly taking part in a scavenger hunt. The invitations themselves had been carefully crafted with coded messages, subtle hints about their past transgressions—little nudges to unsettle them. She imagined the uncomfortable glances, the whispers, as they tried to figure out who knew what.

The second part, more sinister in its execution, involved personal objects hidden throughout the mansion—photographs, letters, artifacts linked to their darkest secrets. These "treasures" were clues to an overarching mystery only Anastacia knew the answer to. The thrill of watching her guests unravel as they discovered these artifacts would be exquisite. Every time they believed they were getting closer to the truth, she would lead them further into a labyrinth of lies.

Her eyes drifted to the antique mirror in the corner of her study. Isabelle had insisted she keep it in her room, going on about its "special properties." Anastacia had initially scoffed at the idea, but lately, she had found herself avoiding the mirror entirely. She couldn't explain why, but every time she caught her reflection, something felt wrong. It was as if the image in the mirror wasn't quite her, or perhaps, it was her, but a version of herself that was slipping further away from reality.

She rose from her chair and approached the mirror cautiously. The frame was gilded, ornate, its surface so polished it seemed to glow in the dim light. She stared at her reflection, but the longer she looked, the more unsettling it became. Her face seemed to distort, shift, as though the mirror was showing her not as she was, but as she would become—a twisted, hollow version of herself.

Shuddering, she turned away, forcing her thoughts back to the party preparations.

Party Preparation: The Scavenger Hunt and Mind Games

The following days were consumed by preparations for the party. Anastacia's mansion buzzed with activity as staff rushed to ensure that every detail was perfect. But amidst the florists, decorators, and caterers, Anastacia maintained an air of detachment. This wasn't just a party; it was a chess game, and her guests were pawns.

Caroline, her personal assistant, was instrumental in coordinating the more complex elements of the scavenger hunt. Together, they devised intricate riddles that required an understanding of both the house and its history. Some clues would lead guests into hidden rooms; others would take them to the more eerie sections of the mansion that most avoided. Anastacia's favorite clue involved the cryptic phrase: The reflection hides the truth, but only when the light is dim.

The idea was simple. At a certain point during the evening, the lighting in the mansion would subtly shift, casting long shadows that would distort the appearance of certain mirrors. The guests, by now sufficiently unnerved, would be drawn to these mirrors, only to find symbols appearing in the glass—symbols they couldn't explain.

Even more entertaining would be the discovery of personal objects—pieces of the guests' own lives Anastacia had collected over the years. A handkerchief embroidered with initials, a broken watch, an old love letter—items that spoke of past indiscretions and secrets. Placed strategically throughout the mansion, each artifact would be a clue, though they wouldn't immediately realize that these clues were connected to them. She could already see their faces when realization struck, when they understood that someone had been watching them all along.

Caroline approached Anastacia with a list of final details, her calm efficiency a balm to Anastacia's fraying nerves.

"Everything is in place," Caroline said, handing her a file. "The guest list has been confirmed, and the staff knows to follow your lead. If any of the guests seem unsettled, we'll redirect them to the next clue."

Anastacia nodded, her mind already moving beyond logistics to the larger picture. This party wasn't just a celebration of her life—it was a reckoning for those who had wronged her. Every person invited had a role to play, whether they knew it or not.

The mansion had always affected Nathaniel differently than it did Anastacia. Where she saw opportunity and power, he saw shadows and whispers. His paranoia had been growing for weeks, his fragile mind deteriorating under the weight of whatever haunted him.

In the dead of night, Anastacia often heard him moving through the halls, muttering to himself. His obsession with the mansion's history—particularly the rumors of their family's curse—had become all-consuming. He had started keeping a journal, meticulously documenting every strange occurrence, every dark dream.

Anastacia had found the journal one morning, left carelessly on the dining table. She had leafed through it, her eyes narrowing at the disjointed entries. Nathaniel's handwriting had become erratic, his thoughts more fragmented with each passing day.

Journal Entry: Nathaniel Graves

The walls are closing in. I hear them every night—the footsteps, the voices. They're coming closer. I thought it was just in my head at first, but now I know. The house is alive. It's watching us. Watching me. I can feel it in my bones. Anastacia doesn't believe me. She never did. But the truth is here. It's always been here, buried beneath the lies we've told ourselves. Father knew. That's why he built this place the way he did. He knew what the house was capable of. The shadows are growing longer, darker. Sometimes, when I look in the mirror, I see someone else staring back at me. It's not me. It's never been me.

They're coming for us. The past is catching up. And when it does, none of us will survive.

Anastacia had closed the journal abruptly, unease prickling at the back of her neck. Nathaniel had always been prone to paranoia, but this was something different. This was madness.

She had confronted him later that day, demanding to know what he was talking about in his journal, but he had only stared at her, his eyes hollow, his skin pale and clammy.

"You don't understand," he had whispered. "The mansion… it's waking up. It's been waiting for this."

Waiting for what?

He had refused to answer, retreating further into his obsession. Anastacia had dismissed his ramblings at first, chalking them up to stress and his naturally anxious disposition. But as the days passed, and the strange occurrences in the house grew more frequent, she began to wonder if there was some truth to his paranoia.

Marcus arrived at the mansion two days before the party. His presence unsettled Anastacia in a way she hadn't anticipated. She had expected him to be a player in her game, but now that he was here, she felt the balance of power shift. There was something different about Marcus—something darker, more calculating. He wasn't just a pawn in her plan; he had his own agenda, and she wasn't sure what it was.

They hadn't spoken much since his arrival. He moved through the house like a shadow, watching her, always one step behind. There was a tension between them that hadn't existed before, a simmering resentment that neither of them acknowledged.

That evening, as the storm raged outside, they found themselves alone in the drawing room. The fire crackled in the hearth, casting flickering shadows on the walls. Anastacia sat by the window, staring out at the rain, while Marcus stood by the fireplace, his gaze fixed on her.

"You've changed," Marcus said, breaking the silence.

Anastacia didn't look at him. "We've all changed."

He took a step closer, his voice soft but insistent. "This isn't about the party, is it? This is about control. It always has been."

She turned to face him, her eyes cold. "And what if it is? You knew who I was when you came here."

Marcus smiled, but it didn't reach his eyes. "You think you're in control, but you're not. Not anymore."

She felt a surge of anger at his words. Marcus had always known how to push her buttons, how to make her feel vulnerable. But she wouldn't let him get to her. Not this time. "You're wrong," she said, standing up and crossing the room to face him. "I'm always in control."

He reached out, brushing a strand of hair from her face, his touch lingering longer than necessary. "Not this time, Anastacia. This time, the house is in control."

She slapped his hand away, her heart racing. "I don't need you, Marcus. I never did."

Marcus laughed softly, a bitter edge to his voice. "Keep telling yourself that."

They stood there for a moment, locked in a silent battle of wills. The tension between them was palpable, thick with unresolved feelings and unspoken words. But before either of them could say anything more, the sound of footsteps echoed down the hallway.

The footsteps grew louder, more deliberate, as though someone—or something—was approaching. Marcus tensed, his eyes darting to the door, but Anastacia remained still, her gaze drifting once again to the mirror in the corner of the room.

The mirror had been in the mansion for as long as she could remember. Isabelle, a family friend with a penchant for the

occult, had insisted that the mirror held special properties—
that it was a gateway of sorts, a conduit between worlds. At
the time, Anastacia had dismissed Isabelle's claims as the
ramblings of an eccentric old woman, but now, she wasn't
so sure.

Lately, the mirror had taken on a new significance. It seemed
to pulse with a dark energy, its surface distorting whenever
she looked into it. She had avoided it for weeks, but now,
standing here in the drawing room with Marcus, she felt an
inexplicable pull toward it.

"Isabelle was right about the mirror," Marcus said quietly, as
if reading her thoughts. "It's more than just a reflection. It
shows us what we want to see… and what we don't."

Anastacia's heart pounded in her chest. "You're talking
nonsense."

"Am I?" Marcus stepped closer to the mirror, his reflection
distorted and twisted in the glass. "Look closer, Anastacia.
You'll see it too."

She hesitated, fear gnawing at the edges of her mind. But
curiosity won out, and she found herself moving toward the
mirror, her breath shallow as she stared into its depths.

At first, all she saw was her own reflection—pale, tired, but
unmistakably her. But as she looked closer, the image began

to shift, the edges blurring and twisting until she saw something else.

A figure stood behind her, cloaked in shadow, its eyes glowing red in the darkness.

Anastacia gasped, stumbling back from the mirror, her heart racing. "What the hell—"

Marcus didn't react. He only watched her, his expression unreadable. "It's not just a mirror, Anastacia. It's a door."

"A door to what?" she demanded, her voice shaking.

"To the truth."

The Party Begins: Countdown of Shadows

The night of the party arrived, and the mansion was bathed in candlelight, the storm outside continuing to rage. The guests arrived one by one, dressed in their finest, unaware of the game they were about to play.

Anastacia greeted them with a smile, her heart pounding with anticipation. Everything was in place. The clues, the mirrors, the scavenger hunt. All of it leading to one inevitable conclusion.

As the guests mingled, sipping champagne and exchanging pleasantries, Anastacia watched them closely. They had no idea what was coming. No idea that by the end of the night, their darkest secrets would be laid bare.

The clock struck midnight, and the first clue was revealed.

Chapter 5

The Dance of Deception

The night of the masquerade ball had finally arrived, and the mansion hummed with a strange, almost sentient anticipation. The air inside was heavy, as though the walls themselves were holding their breath, waiting for what was to come. Outside, the storm that had been building for days raged with fury, the wind howling like a beast denied entry. The mansion stood resolute, its ancient stone walls seeming to pulse in time with the thunder, as if alive with the same dark energy that had been swirling around its inhabitants.

Anastacia stood at the top of the grand staircase, her mask in place—a delicate, black lace creation that obscured her eyes but left her mouth free, the better to smile with calculated charm. She wore a gown of deep burgundy, the fabric clinging to her curves like blood on skin. She could feel the weight of the night pressing down on her, but she welcomed it. This was her stage, her moment to orchestrate a night of revelation and reckoning. Every guest would play their part, whether they realized it or not.

Below her, the ballroom was a sea of masked faces. Glittering chandeliers cast a golden glow over the scene, their light refracted by crystal prisms, creating the illusion of countless stars dancing in the shadows. The guests moved in swirling patterns, their laughter and conversation an undercurrent to the more dangerous currents running beneath the surface. Each of them wore a mask, not just on their faces, but over their lives—hiding secrets, lies, and betrayals that would soon be exposed.

The masquerade was everything Anastacia had envisioned. The ballroom was transformed into a place of mystery and deception, where nothing was as it seemed. Each guest had been carefully chosen, each costume reflective of who they were—or who they wanted others to believe they were. There was Geraldine, the elegant widow draped in mourning attire, whose late husband's sudden and suspicious death was whispered about in elite circles. Michael, the suave businessman whose polished exterior hid his crumbling empire. Even Caroline, Anastacia's personal assistant, moved among the guests in a silver gown, looking every bit as formidable as the secrets she kept for her employer.

The masks lent an air of secrecy to the night, but Anastacia knew that by the end, no one would be able to hide behind them.

Anastacia's Entrance: The Games Begin

Anastacia descended the staircase slowly, her entrance drawing the attention of the crowd. Eyes followed her every move, though none dared approach her immediately. She was the queen of this night, and she knew it. She reveled in the power she felt in those moments, the control she had over them all—over their fates, their emotions, their secrets.

At the base of the staircase, she was greeted by a flurry of compliments, admiring glances, and veiled whispers. She smiled graciously, but her mind was already on the games she had set in motion. Her guests believed they had been invited to celebrate her 50th birthday in style, but in reality, they were the pawns in a far more intricate game.

Each of them had received an invitation bearing a clue—an enigmatic puzzle designed to unsettle them. The scavenger hunt would take them deeper into the mansion, where hidden truths waited to be uncovered. And each truth was a piece of the larger puzzle, leading them toward a revelation none of them were prepared for.

As Anastacia moved through the crowd, she caught snippets of conversation—whispers of confusion, speculation about the night's events. Her guests were already on edge, their nerves frayed by the storm outside and the cryptic nature of her invitations. Exactly as she had planned.

Nathaniel stood near the far wall, his mask a simple black half-face that did little to hide his furrowed brow and tense posture. He had been watching Anastacia all night, his gaze like a hawk's—sharp and unblinking. He was waiting, always waiting, for the inevitable collapse. His paranoia had grown worse over the past few weeks, and though he tried to mask it with quiet words and reassuring glances, Anastacia could see the fear gnawing at him. The mansion had gotten to him, as it always did.

She approached him slowly, her smile sharp as a blade. "Enjoying the party, Nathaniel?"

He barely looked at her, his eyes darting over the crowd as if searching for threats. "You should stop this," he murmured under his breath. "It's not too late."

Anastacia tilted her head, feigning confusion. "Stop what? It's just a party."

He turned to face her, his eyes dark and serious behind the mask. "This isn't a game, Anastacia. You're playing with forces you don't understand."

She laughed softly, a sound that held no humor. "You always say that. What forces, Nathaniel? The mansion? The family curse? Or is it me you're afraid of?"

His jaw clenched, and for a moment, she thought he might walk away. But then he leaned in close, his voice barely a whisper. "You think you're in control, but you're not. The house knows. It's always known."

Anastacia's smile faltered for a brief second before she regained her composure. "If the house knows, then let it watch. I have nothing to hide."

Nathaniel opened his mouth to respond, but before he could say anything, a loud laugh echoed from across the room. Anastacia's gaze shifted, and she saw Marcus standing near the entrance, a drink in his hand, his eyes locked onto hers from across the ballroom. His mask was white, featureless, giving him an almost ghostly appearance against the vibrant colors of the other guests. There was something dangerous in his posture, something that set her nerves on edge.

The evening progressed as Anastacia had envisioned—whispers growing louder, unease spreading through the crowd like a slow poison. She moved from group to group, dropping hints, planting seeds of doubt. She knew exactly which buttons to press, which lies to expose just enough to make her guests squirm.

Geraldine, the widow, had been gossiping with another guest when Anastacia casually mentioned the name of Geraldine's deceased husband's business partner—a man who had disappeared under suspicious circumstances shortly after the husband's death. Geraldine's face had gone pale, her eyes darting around the room as if searching for an escape. Anastacia had smiled sweetly, offering her a glass of champagne as though nothing was amiss.

Michael, the businessman, had been boasting about a recent deal when Anastacia leaned in close and whispered, "I heard your company's been losing millions. How are you managing to keep it all under wraps?" His hand had tightened around his glass, a flicker of panic crossing his face before he composed himself with a forced laugh.

The night was a game of psychological warfare, and Anastacia was the master of it.

But as the evening wore on, she began to sense something else at play—something beyond her control. The mansion had always been an extension of her power, but tonight it felt… different. The walls seemed to pulse with an energy she couldn't quite place, the air heavy with tension that had nothing to do with her guests' secrets.

Marcus had been circling her all night, his presence like a shadow she couldn't shake. He was watching her, always watching, waiting for the right moment to strike.

When he finally approached her, it was with the same disarming smile he had always used to get what he wanted.

"You look stunning," Marcus said, his voice smooth but with an edge that made her uneasy.

"Thank you," Anastacia replied, her smile thin. "You clean up well yourself."

He took a sip of his drink, his eyes never leaving hers. "Is this your way of making amends, Anastacia? Throwing a grand party to remind us all of the good old days?"

She raised an eyebrow, her defenses snapping into place. "Amends for what, Marcus? I don't recall owing anyone an apology."

His lips curled into a smile, but it didn't reach his eyes. "No, you never do, do you?"

The tension between them crackled like electricity, drawing the attention of those nearby. Conversations hushed, eyes turning toward the pair as the air in the room grew thick with anticipation.

Before Anastacia could respond, the lights flickered, and the chandelier above them swayed slightly. The music faltered for a moment, replaced by a low, almost imperceptible hum that seemed to resonate from deep within the walls of the mansion. The crowd shifted uneasily, murmurs of confusion rippling through the ballroom.

Anastacia's breath hitched, her gaze darting around the room. The mansion was reacting—just as it had in the past few weeks. Every time the tension between her and someone else reached a certain peak, the house seemed to respond, as though feeding off the energy they created.

She forced a smile, her voice steady despite the unease creeping up her spine. "It's just the storm. Nothing to worry about."

Marcus didn't seem convinced. His eyes narrowed, and he took a step closer, lowering his voice. "Do you feel it, Anastacia? The house… it's alive tonight."

Her stomach tightened, but she refused to let him see her fear. "Don't be ridiculous, Marcus."

He leaned in, his breath warm against her ear. "You can lie to everyone else, but you can't lie to me. You feel it, just like I do."

The lights flickered again, and this time, they stayed off for a few heartbeats too long. In the darkness, Anastacia could hear the guests murmuring, their unease growing. When the lights returned, everything seemed just a little bit off—the shadows deeper, the air colder, the weight of the night pressing down harder.

She glanced toward the staircase and saw Isabelle standing at the top, her mask a grotesque creation of dark feathers and twisted metal. She held a single candle, the flame flickering in the draught that seemed to follow her like a cloak.

Isabelle's eyes found Anastacia's, and for a moment, everything else faded away. There was something knowing in Isabelle's gaze, something ancient and dangerous.

As the guests continued their uneasy conversations, Geraldine wandered away from the main group, her nerves frayed after Anastacia's not-so-subtle reminder of her past. She found herself drawn toward a large, ornate mirror in the corner of the room—one Anastacia had specifically placed there as part of the scavenger hunt.

The mirror was draped in a heavy black cloth, but something compelled Geraldine to pull it away. The moment she did, her reflection stared back at her—but it wasn't her. The woman in the mirror wore the same mask and gown, but her face was younger, her eyes filled with a fear Geraldine recognized all too well.

It was her—twenty years ago—the night of her husband's death.

She gasped, stumbling back from the mirror, her heart racing. The woman in the reflection didn't move, didn't blink. She just stared, accusingly.

Geraldine's scream echoed through the ballroom, drawing the attention of the other guests. Anastacia turned just in time to see her collapse to the floor, her mask askew, her face pale as death.

Nathaniel rushed to her side, his expression grim. "She's dead."

The ballroom erupted into chaos. Guests screamed, some running for the doors, others frozen in shock. The chandeliers above swayed violently, the lights flickering in time with the storm outside. The mansion groaned, its walls creaking as though reacting to the death within its walls.

Anastacia stood motionless, her mind racing. This wasn't part of the plan. The scavenger hunt was supposed to be a game, a way to toy with her guests, to make them question their own lies. But now, someone was dead, and the mansion was alive with a malevolent energy she could no longer ignore.

She turned to find Marcus, but he was gone. The crowd surged around her, panic spreading like wildfire, and for the first time that night, Anastacia felt truly afraid. The mansion had taken control, and there was nothing she could do to stop it.

And then, from somewhere deep within the house, she heard the voice again.

"This is your story, Anastacia. But you are not the author.

Chapter 6

Nightfall of Betrayal

The night had spiraled into madness.

The once-lively masquerade ball had devolved into chaos, the mansion's opulent ballroom now a stage for fear and confusion. Guests scrambled through the hallways, their masks discarded, their faces pale with panic. Outside, the storm raged with a fury that felt personal, as if the elements themselves had turned against the people within the mansion. The wind screamed through the cracks in the ancient stone walls, rattling the windows and shaking the chandeliers above.

Anastacia stood at the center of the grand staircase, her pulse pounding in her ears. Her guests—her friends, acquaintances, and enemies—were running, their footsteps echoing through the vast, darkened halls of the mansion. But she couldn't move. She was frozen in place, her mind a whirlpool of fragmented thoughts. The death of the woman at the masquerade was not part of her plan. Nothing that had happened tonight was part of her plan.

"This is your story, Anastacia, but you are not the author."

The words, whispered like a prayer or a curse, echoed in her mind, refusing to fade. The voice—so close, yet so impossible—was like a presence, lingering just beyond her sight. Every time she thought she was alone, it would appear, a ghostly reminder that she had lost control.

Behind her mask, her face was a mask of its own—stunned, blank, struggling to comprehend what was happening. Her carefully constructed world, built on secrets, lies, and the illusion of control, was crumbling around her. She could feel it slipping through her fingers, like sand in an hourglass, with no way to stop it.

The mansion groaned, its walls shifting with a life of their own, as if the house was breathing, watching. Anastacia knew that the others felt it too. She had seen it in their eyes during the ball—the way they glanced at the shadows, the way they flinched when the lights flickered. The mansion had come alive tonight, responding to the rising tension, feeding on their fear.

The ballroom had become a scene of pandemonium, its once-elegant atmosphere replaced by an air of desperation and terror. Geraldine, pale and trembling, clung to her husband as they tried to find their way out of the labyrinthine mansion. Their laughter had turned to gasps of terror after witnessing the woman's sudden death, her lifeless body sprawled across the dance floor like some kind of twisted offering to the house.

Michael, the businessman, was pacing near the grand windows, his face drawn in tight lines as he muttered under his breath about the storm. His mask was gone, thrown aside in his frantic attempt to escape the mounting dread. "This is insane," he kept saying. "There's got to be a way out."

The chandeliers overhead swayed ominously as the storm raged on outside, casting erratic shadows across the floor. Glasses shattered on the ground as guests bumped into tables and each other, their once-graceful movements now a chaotic dance of survival.

"I need to get out of here," one guest shouted, their voice cracking. Others echoed the sentiment, but every attempt to leave was thwarted. The mansion, as if sensing their desperation, seemed to conspire against them. Doors that should have led to exits were locked, or worse—led them into unfamiliar rooms they hadn't entered before. The house was changing, warping, trapping them in its clutches.

Each guest reacted differently to the madness. Caroline, the efficient assistant, kept her calm as she tried to lead a small group through the corridors, but even her carefully maintained composure was starting to fray at the edges.

"This place is playing tricks on us," she muttered, her voice tight with frustration.

Some guests tried to break the windows, hoping to flee into the storm outside, but the glass wouldn't shatter. It was as though the mansion had sealed itself from the outside world, determined to keep them within.

The house seemed to relish the bloodshed. Anastacia could feel it in her bones—the shift in the air, the way the walls groaned and creaked in a language only the house understood. The death at the masquerade had triggered something, awakening the mansion in a way she had never anticipated. The very structure of the house seemed to shift and breathe, warping as though reacting to the terror and confusion within its walls.

Objects began to move on their own. Small, subtle at first— books sliding off shelves, curtains swaying despite the windows being closed. But soon, the movements became more pronounced. Chairs scraped across the floor of their own accord, doors slammed shut without warning, and mirrors distorted the reflections they held.

One guest, a woman named Julia, gasped as she passed by a large mirror in the dining hall. For a moment, her reflection didn't match her movements. She stopped in front of the mirror, watching in horror as the reflection of herself smiled, though her own lips remained still. "Help me," the reflection mouthed, and Julia stumbled backward, her heart hammering in her chest. She ran from the room, her screams joining the cacophony of panic that now filled the mansion.

The house was playing with them. Anastacia could feel it in the way the floors shifted beneath her feet, the way the walls seemed to close in, confining them all within its grasp. There was no logic to the layout of the rooms anymore—corridors that should have led to the foyer twisted and turned into endless loops, trapping those who tried to leave.

As she moved through the mansion, Anastacia realized that the house was not just reacting to the chaos—it was feeding off it, growing stronger with each passing moment. The air felt thicker, heavier, as though the mansion was drawing power from the fear and confusion of the guests.

Amidst the chaos, the sound of pounding on the front door cut through the madness. It was jarring, the sudden noise of someone from the outside world trying to gain entry to the madness within. For a brief moment, there was hope— perhaps someone had come to rescue them.

Anastacia rushed toward the foyer, pushing her way through the guests who had crowded near the door, desperate for an escape. Her heart raced as she reached the door, pulling it open to reveal two police officers, their faces grim as they stepped inside, taking in the scene before them.

"Anastacia Graves?" one of the officers asked, his voice low and authoritative.

"Yes," Anastacia replied, her voice wavering slightly. "There's been an accident."

The officer's eyes narrowed as he glanced around the room, taking in the panicked guests, the overturned furniture, and the unmistakable tension that hung in the air. "We received a report about a death at this location."

Anastacia nodded, swallowing hard. "A woman… she collapsed during the ball. I don't know what happened."

The officer exchanged a glance with his partner, their expressions grim. "We'll need to ask you and your guests some questions. And we'll need to see the body."

Anastacia's stomach churned as she led the officers toward the ballroom, where the body of the woman still lay motionless on the floor. The guests had retreated to the edges of the room, whispering among themselves as the officers knelt beside the body, their faces impassive as they examined her.

But even as the investigation began, Anastacia knew that there was more at play here than a simple death. The mansion was alive, and it wasn't finished with them yet.

As the officers worked to secure the scene and question the guests, Anastacia's thoughts turned to Henry's death. The sight of his body, twisted and lifeless in the library, was still fresh in her mind. She had done everything she could to cover her tracks, to make sure no one would ever suspect the truth behind his death. But now, with law enforcement in the mansion, she couldn't help but wonder if she had missed something.

Her mind raced as she considered her next move. She needed to ensure that the officers didn't dig too deeply into Henry's death. She couldn't let them discover the truth—not with the mansion watching her every move, waiting for her to slip up. As the officers questioned the guests, Anastacia made her way back to the library, her heart pounding in her chest. The room was just as she had left it—dark, cold, and silent. Henry's body was gone, but the bloodstains on the floor remained, a stark reminder of what had happened.

She knelt beside the spot where Henry had fallen, her fingers brushing against the dried blood. The memory of his death played out in her mind, vivid and brutal. She had thought she could control the situation, but now, as the mansion seemed to conspire against her, she realized just how little control she had.

The word LIAR still haunted her. It had been scrawled in Henry's blood, an accusation that felt as though it had been aimed directly at her. Was it the mansion's way of revealing her secrets? Or was there something else at work—something darker, more sinister?

As she stood in the library, lost in thought, the door creaked open behind her. She turned sharply, her heart leaping into her throat as she saw one of the officers standing in the doorway, his expression unreadable.

"Ms. Graves," he said, his voice low and steady. "We need to ask you a few questions about Henry Lawson."

Anastacia's blood ran cold. She had been so careful—how could they possibly know?

The officer's questioning was interrupted by a sudden, violent shudder that ran through the mansion. The walls groaned, the floor beneath their feet shifting as though the house itself was alive and reacting to the investigation. Books tumbled from the shelves, furniture scraped across the floor, and a chill filled the room, as if the mansion was warning them to stop.

Anastacia's heart raced as the lights flickered, plunging the library into darkness for several long moments. When the lights returned, the officer was staring at her, his expression wary. He had felt it too—whatever force was at play here, it wasn't just her imagination.

"I don't know what's happening," Anastacia whispered, her voice trembling.

The officer stepped closer, his gaze sharp. "This house… there's something wrong with it, isn't there?"

Before Anastacia could answer, the room seemed to shift around them. The bookshelves that had lined the walls were now gone, replaced by solid stone. The door they had entered through was no longer there. The mansion had changed again, trapping them in a room that no longer existed in the layout of the house.

Panic surged through Anastacia as she realized that the mansion was reacting to the investigation—twisting itself to prevent anyone from uncovering its secrets. The officer was visibly shaken, his confidence slipping as he looked around the room in disbelief.

"What the hell is going on?" he demanded, his voice rising in panic.

Anastacia didn't have an answer. All she knew was that the mansion was alive, and it was protecting itself from whatever they were trying to uncover.

As the investigation continued, the mansion's behavior grew more erratic. Guests reported seeing objects move on their own—chairs sliding across the floor, paintings tilting on the walls, and even the chandeliers swaying despite the absence of wind.

One guest claimed to have seen a door appear where there hadn't been one before, only for it to vanish as soon as they approached it. Others swore they heard whispers coming from the walls, though no one could make out what was being said.

The layout of the mansion had become a living puzzle. Hallways that had once led to the ballroom now twisted and turned into unfamiliar rooms. Guests found themselves lost in parts of the mansion they had never seen before, despite having been there only hours earlier.

Anastacia could feel the mansion's power growing with each passing moment. It was as though the house was feeding off the fear and confusion of the guests, drawing strength from their panic. The walls seemed to pulse with a dark energy, the air thick with the weight of the supernatural forces at play.

As the night wore on, Anastacia realized that she was no longer in control of the situation. The mansion had taken over, bending reality to its will. The death at the masquerade, Henry's murder, the investigation—none of it had gone as she had planned. The house had its own agenda, and she was merely a pawn in its game.

She had thought she could control the narrative, that she could manipulate the events to suit her needs. But now, standing in the heart of the mansion, surrounded by chaos and fear, she understood the truth.

She wasn't the author of this story.

The mansion was.

And it wasn't finished with her yet.

"

Part III:

Echoes of the Unwritten

Chapter 7

The Spiral Unseen

The mansion groaned, its walls creaking as though they were alive and slowly, deliberately, closing in on Anastacia. The storm outside raged with a vengeance, battering the windows with sheets of rain that lashed against the glass like a relentless onslaught. But inside the mansion, the storm was quieter—darker, more dangerous. It was a storm of fear and paranoia, of shadows that seemed to move just out of sight and whispers that echoed through the halls, barely audible but always present.

Anastacia stood in the center of the ballroom, her body frozen in place as the figure loomed before her. It didn't move. It didn't speak. It simply stood there, its dark form like a shadow made flesh, its presence suffocating. She could feel its gaze on her—though she couldn't see its face—and that gaze was like a weight pressing down on her chest, making it impossible to breathe.

The guests behind her were in disarray, some cowering in the corners, others whispering frantically to one another, their fear palpable. No one dared to approach the figure, and no one dared to speak above a whisper, as though the very sound of their voices might draw its attention.

Anastacia's mind raced. The figure had been in the mirror—she had seen it there, watching her. And now it was here, real and solid and impossibly close. She had always prided herself on her ability to stay in control, to command any situation with ease, but now… now she felt that control slipping through her fingers like sand.

She took a step back, her breath coming in shallow, ragged gasps. The figure didn't follow her. It remained where it stood, silent and still, but its presence was overwhelming. Every instinct screamed at her to run, to get as far away from it as possible, but her legs refused to obey. She was trapped, frozen in place by a fear so deep it felt like a physical force holding her there.

A hand suddenly gripped her shoulder, jerking her out of her paralysis. She spun around, her heart hammering in her chest, and found herself face-to-face with Nathaniel. His eyes were wide with terror, his face pale beneath his mask.

"We have to go," he whispered, his voice trembling. "We have to get out of here. Now."

Anastacia's gaze flicked back to the figure. It hadn't moved, but she could feel its attention on her, like an invisible hand reaching out to grasp her.

"I can't," she whispered back, her voice barely audible.

"Yes, you can," Nathaniel insisted, his grip tightening on her shoulder. "Please, Anastacia, we have to leave. The house… it's alive. It's feeding off of us. You've felt it too. You know it."

She did know it. She had felt it for weeks, the subtle shift in the air, the way the shadows seemed deeper, more alive than they should be. But she had refused to acknowledge it. She had dismissed Nathaniel's warnings, brushed off the strange occurrences as nothing more than coincidences. Now, standing here in the ballroom with the figure looming before her, she couldn't deny it any longer.

The mansion was alive.

But more than that, it was hungry.

Anastacia swallowed hard, forcing herself to take a deep breath. She had to regain control. She couldn't let this break her. She couldn't let this thing win. She had spent her entire life building herself up, becoming the woman who could control her own destiny, and she wasn't about to let some supernatural force take that away from her.

"I'm not running," she said, her voice firming as she stepped away from Nathaniel. "This is my house. My life. I'm not going to let it win."

Nathaniel stared at her, disbelief written across his face. "You don't understand, Anastacia. It's too late. The house has already claimed us."

"No," she snapped, her eyes blazing with determination. "It hasn't. I won't let it."

Without waiting for his response, Anastacia turned and strode toward the ballroom doors, her heels clicking sharply against the marble floor. The figure remained where it stood, but she could feel its gaze following her, a cold, invisible presence that sent shivers down her spine. She refused to look back at it. She refused to acknowledge the fear that gnawed at the edges of her mind.

The guests watched her as she passed, their faces a mixture of fear and disbelief. No one dared to speak, no one dared to follow. They were paralyzed by their own terror, their eyes wide and unblinking behind their masks.

Anastacia reached the doors and pushed them open with a forceful shove. The hallway beyond was dark, the only light coming from the flickering candles that lined the walls, casting long shadows that twisted and danced like living things. She stepped into the hallway, the doors swinging shut behind her with a heavy thud.

The moment she was alone, the weight of everything crashed down on her.

Her hands trembled as she pressed them against the cool stone walls, trying to steady herself. The mansion felt like it was closing in on her, the walls seeming to pulse with a life of their own. The air was thick, oppressive, and the shadows that clung to the corners of the hallway felt more like entities than mere absence of light.

She could feel it now—the presence of the house, the way it had been watching her, waiting for the perfect moment to strike. It had toyed with her, played games with her mind, slowly stripping away her control piece by piece. And now, it was winning.

But she wasn't going to let it.

Anastacia straightened, her jaw set in grim determination. She had faced worse than this—business rivals who had tried to ruin her, betrayals from those she had trusted. She had survived them all, and she would survive this too.

She pushed off the wall and started down the hallway, her footsteps echoing in the silence. She didn't know where she was going, but she knew she had to keep moving. She had to stay ahead of whatever was lurking in the shadows.

As she walked, the mansion seemed to shift around her. The familiar hallways, the grand rooms she had known for years, felt different now—warped, distorted. Doors that should have led to certain rooms opened into unfamiliar spaces, and the once straight corridors seemed to twist and curve in impossible ways.

It was as if the house was rearranging itself, trapping her in its labyrinthine design.

Panic clawed at her chest, but she forced it down, refusing to give in. She kept walking, her pace quickening as the shadows around her deepened. The flickering candlelight did little to dispel the darkness, and the whispers—the same faint, eerie whispers she had been hearing for weeks—grew louder, more insistent.

"It's coming."

"You can't escape."

"This is your fate."

Anastacia clenched her fists, her nails digging into her palms. The voices were trying to get into her head, trying to break her. But she wouldn't let them. She had spent her entire life building walls around herself, walls that no one could breach, and she wasn't about to let some haunted mansion tear them down.

She turned a corner, her heart racing, and stopped dead in her tracks.

Ahead of her, standing at the end of the hallway, was the figure.

It hadn't moved. It hadn't followed her. It had simply… appeared.

Her breath caught in her throat, her body frozen in place. The figure was closer now, its features still obscured by darkness, but its presence was even more overwhelming. The air around it seemed to ripple, distorting the space like a heat mirage, and the shadows clung to it like a cloak.

Anastacia's mind screamed at her to run, but her body refused to obey. She was trapped, caught in the figure's gaze, her heart pounding in her chest like a drumbeat.

And then, the figure spoke.

Its voice was low, a whisper that echoed through the hallway, but it was clear, unmistakable.

"You're not in control, Anastacia."

Her stomach twisted, the words hitting her like a physical blow. She shook her head, her lips parting to protest, but no sound came out.

"You never were," the figure continued, its voice soft, almost soothing. "You thought you could command this place, bend it to your will. But the house has always been in control."

Anastacia took a step back, her heart racing. "That's not true," she whispered, her voice trembling. "I built this. I made it mine."

The figure's laugh was soft, almost mocking. "You built nothing. You're just a pawn, Anastacia. And now the house will claim what it's owed."

The shadows around the figure seemed to pulse, stretching out toward her like dark tendrils, reaching for her. She stumbled back, her pulse pounding in her ears as she fought to regain control, to push the fear away.

But it was no use. The figure was right.

She had lost control.

The house had always been in control.

And now it was coming for her.

Anastacia woke with a start, her breath coming in shallow gasps, her heart pounding in her chest. She was back in her bedroom, the familiar surroundings of her private sanctuary a stark contrast to the nightmare she had just lived through.

But was it a nightmare? Or had it been real?

She sat up in bed, her body trembling as she looked around the room. Everything was as it should be—her elegant furnishings, the warm glow of the fireplace, the heavy velvet curtains that draped the windows. But the air still felt thick, oppressive, and she could hear the faint echo of the figure's voice in her mind.

"You're not in control."

She pressed a hand to her chest, trying to calm her racing heart. It had to be a dream. It had to be. But the fear clung to her, wrapping around her like a shroud.

For the first time in her life, Anastacia felt truly powerless.

As the night wore on, Anastacia's mind spiraled further. The mansion seemed to press down on her, its presence growing stronger, more malevolent. She tried to focus on practical matters—what to do about Henry's death, how to manage the terrified guests—but her thoughts were muddled, her control slipping away with every passing hour.

She wandered the mansion, her footsteps echoing through the empty halls. The guests had retreated to their rooms, too afraid to continue the party, and the mansion was eerily quiet now, save for the ever-present hum of the storm outside.

But even in the silence, Anastacia could hear the whispers. They were faint, just on the edge of her hearing, but they were there, always there.

"You're not in control."

"The house is alive."

"It's coming for you."

By the time dawn approached, Anastacia was a shell of the woman she had once been. Her perfectly curated life, her carefully constructed empire—it all felt meaningless now, dwarfed by the overwhelming presence of the mansion. She had thought she could control it, bend it to her will, but now she realized the truth.

The house had been in control all along.

And it had been waiting for her.

Anastacia's mind was still reeling from her encounter with the shadowy figure when she realized Nathaniel was gone. He had been right beside her, his hand gripping her arm, urging her to leave the mansion. Now, she was alone in the dim hallway, the flickering candlelight casting eerie shadows on the walls.

Panic surged through her. Nathaniel might have been paranoid, but he was still her brother. She couldn't lose him. Not like this. She turned on her heel, her heels clicking loudly on the floor as she hurried down the hall, calling out his name.

"Nathaniel? Nathaniel!"

Her voice echoed through the silent mansion, but there was no response. The silence felt unnatural, heavy, like the mansion was deliberately swallowing up the sound, mocking her efforts to find him. She could feel the mansion's presence again, wrapping around her like a cold fog, making it difficult to think clearly.

Flashbacks of Nathaniel's recent behavior flooded her mind as she moved deeper into the mansion, the hallways stretching endlessly before her, twisting and turning in ways that defied logic. Nathaniel had always been sensitive, always prone to anxiety and fear, but in the weeks leading up to tonight, something had shifted in him. He had become more erratic, more desperate, as if he knew something no one else did.

The memory was sharp and clear.

It had been a few days before the party, and Anastacia had found Nathaniel pacing in the library, his face pale, his eyes bloodshot. His hands had been shaking as he clutched a worn journal—Eleanor Glenoire's journal, the one he had found in the attic. His breath came in ragged gasps, and he looked like a man on the verge of collapse.

"Anastacia, you have to listen to me," he had pleaded, his voice trembling. "The house—it's not just old. It's alive. It's been feeding on us for years."

Anastacia had rolled her eyes at him, as she always did when he got like this. "Nathaniel, you're being ridiculous. It's just a house. You're letting that old journal get into your head."

But Nathaniel had been insistent, more than usual. His eyes, usually filled with doubt and fear, had held something different this time. Something more desperate. "You don't understand," he had whispered, his voice low and urgent. "It's been waiting for us. For our family. We're part of it—

part of whatever curse is tied to this place. And now it's waking up."

Anastacia had dismissed him, brushing off his warnings as the ramblings of a man who had always been afraid of his own shadow. But deep down, a small part of her had felt the same unease. She had felt the shift in the house, the way the air had thickened, the way the shadows seemed to stretch farther than they should. But admitting that would mean admitting that Nathaniel was right, and she couldn't do that. Not then.

Now, the memory felt like a weight on her chest, pressing down on her with the force of her guilt. She had ignored him. She had brushed aside his warnings, and now... now Nathaniel was missing.

Anastacia's pace quickened as she continued down the hall, her heart pounding in her chest. The mansion felt like it was closing in on her, the walls seeming to shift and twist, the floor beneath her feet creaking in ways it hadn't before. She turned a corner, her breath catching in her throat as she caught a glimpse of something—someone—moving just ahead of her.

"Nathaniel!" she called out again, her voice cracking with desperation.

She reached the end of the hallway and found herself standing in front of the door to the attic.

The attic.

It had always been the most unsettling part of the mansion, a place filled with dust-covered relics of the past, forgotten and left to rot. She had avoided it for years, brushing off the strange noises that sometimes echoed from above as nothing more than the settling of the old house. But now, standing in front of the door, she felt a cold dread creep over her. The door was slightly ajar, a sliver of darkness visible through the crack.

Taking a deep breath, Anastacia pushed the door open.

The stairs leading up to the attic were narrow and steep, the wood groaning under her weight as she ascended. The air grew colder the higher she climbed, and the smell of dust and decay filled her lungs. She could hear the faint whisper of wind through the cracks in the walls, but there was something else too—a soft, rhythmic creaking sound, like something swaying back and forth.

When she reached the top, the attic was dimly lit by the moonlight filtering through the small, grimy windows. The space was filled with old furniture, covered in dusty sheets, and boxes stacked haphazardly in every corner. But it was what hung in the center of the room that made Anastacia's blood run cold.

Nathaniel.

He was hanging from a rope, his body swaying gently, the noose tight around his neck. His eyes were wide open, staring blankly at the ceiling, and his face was twisted in an expression of fear and horror. His hands were limp at his sides, the journal—the one he had clung to for weeks—lying on the floor beneath him, its pages splayed open like the final confession of a man who had known too much.

Anastacia's scream echoed through the attic, raw and filled with agony. She rushed toward him, her hands trembling as she tried to undo the rope, to lower him to the ground. But it was too late. Nathaniel was gone.

She crumpled to the floor beside him, her breath coming in shallow gasps, her mind reeling from the sight of her brother's lifeless body. The mansion had taken him. It had finally claimed him, just as he had feared.

"I told you," his voice echoed in her mind, the memory of his desperation filling her thoughts. "It's waking up. It's been waiting for us."

She had ignored him. She had dismissed his warnings, and now she had lost him. He had been right all along, and now the weight of that realization pressed down on her like a crushing wave.

The last time Anastacia had seen Nathaniel alive, he had been standing at the edge of the grand staircase, his face pale and his eyes wild with fear. He had tried to pull her away from the ballroom, tried to make her leave the mansion with him, but she had refused.

"I'm not running," she had said, her voice filled with defiance. "This is my house."

Nathaniel had looked at her then, a look of such sadness and desperation that it had shaken her, though she hadn't shown it. "It's too late," he had whispered. "You think you can control this, but you can't. The house… it's already won."

And then he had disappeared into the darkness of the mansion, his footsteps echoing down the empty halls.

She hadn't followed him.

She had let him go, thinking he was just being paranoid, thinking he would come back when he had calmed down. But now, standing here in the attic with his lifeless body hanging before her, she realized how wrong she had been.

Nathaniel had known. He had known from the beginning that the mansion was alive, that it was feeding off their family, off their fear, off their very souls. And now it had taken him, just as it had taken so many before him.

Anastacia's hands trembled as she reached for the journal on the floor. The pages were filled with Nathaniel's frantic handwriting, his final thoughts, his desperate attempts to understand the curse that had plagued their family for generations.

Nathaniel's Journal

The pages of the journal were stained with tears, the ink smudged in places where Nathaniel's hand had shaken as he wrote. He had been unraveling, his mind fraying at the edges as he tried to make sense of the things he had seen, the things he had felt in the mansion.

"I can hear them," he had written in one of the final entries. "The whispers. They never stop. They tell me things—things about our family, about the curse. They tell me that the house is hungry, that it's been waiting for this moment. For us. For me."

"Anastacia doesn't believe me. She thinks I'm losing my mind. Maybe I am. But I know what I've seen. I know what I've heard. The house is alive, and it wants us. It wants our blood. It's always wanted our blood."

Anastacia's hands shook as she read the final entry, her vision blurring with tears. Nathaniel had been right. He had known all along what the mansion wanted, but she hadn't listened. She had been so focused on maintaining control, on keeping up appearances, that she had ignored the truth staring her in the face.

And now Nathaniel was gone.

As Anastacia knelt beside Nathaniel's lifeless body, the weight of her guilt crushed her, making it hard to breathe. The mansion had claimed him, just as it had claimed so many others before him. It had been waiting—patiently, methodically—for its moment. And now, with Nathaniel gone, Anastacia could feel the house turning its attention toward her.

The journal lay open beside her, its final words haunting her mind:

"There's no escape. The house won't let us leave. It's been feeding on our family for generations, drawing us back here, one by one. And now… it's my turn. I can feel it. I can hear it in the walls, in the very air I breathe. It's coming for me."

The words blurred as tears filled Anastacia's eyes. She had dismissed Nathaniel's fears, had mocked his desperation, and now she realized how wrong she had been. He had tried to warn her, tried to save them both, but she hadn't listened. Now it was too late.

She stood slowly, her legs trembling beneath her. The attic seemed to pulse around her, the air thick and oppressive, pressing down on her from all sides. The shadows danced at the edges of her vision, twisting and writhing like dark tendrils, reaching out for her.

Anastacia knew, in that moment, that the mansion wasn't done with her yet. Nathaniel's death was just the beginning. It had taken him. And now it was coming for her.

With one last look at her brother's lifeless form, Anastacia turned and fled from the attic, her footsteps echoing through the narrow stairwell. She didn't know where she was going, didn't know what she would do, but she knew she couldn't stay in that room any longer. The walls felt like they were closing in on her, suffocating her with the weight of her guilt, her fear, her loss.

As she ran through the darkened hallways of the mansion, the whispers grew louder, more insistent. They were calling her name now, beckoning her deeper into the heart of the house, into the darkness that waited for her.

"You're next, Anastacia. You're next."

The mansion had claimed Nathaniel. And now it was coming for her.

But Anastacia wasn't ready to surrender. Not yet.

With a surge of determination, she pushed the fear down, forced it into the deepest recesses of her mind. She had always been in control, always known how to bend the world to her will. She would survive this, just as she had survived everything else. She had to.

But as the walls seemed to close in around her, and the shadows pressed closer, she couldn't shake the feeling that, this time, the house would win.

Nathaniel's journey had been one of quiet desperation. From the moment he had found Eleanor Glenoire's journal, he had known something was wrong. The mansion had always been a strange, unsettling place, but the journal had revealed a darkness he hadn't been prepared for.

He had spent weeks combing through the pages, piecing together the story of their family's curse. It had started generations ago, a pact made by one of their ancestors, a deal with forces beyond their understanding. The family had prospered, but the price had been steep. Each generation had suffered in its own way, and the mansion had always been at the center of it all.

Nathaniel had felt the weight of that history pressing down on him, and as the days passed, he had become more and more convinced that the mansion was watching them, waiting for the right moment to strike. He had tried to tell

Anastacia, tried to make her understand, but she had brushed him off, just as she always did.

In his final days, the whispers had grown louder. They followed him everywhere—in the hallways, in his bedroom, even in his dreams. He had started to see things, shadowy figures lurking at the edges of his vision, flickers of movement where there should have been none.

And then, on the night of the masquerade, he had realized the truth.

The mansion didn't want to let them go.

He had tried to get Anastacia to leave, had begged her to run, but she had refused. She had been so certain of her control, so sure that she could outmaneuver whatever force was at work in the house.

But Nathaniel had known better.

The mansion had claimed him in the attic, the same place where their ancestor had performed the rituals that had bound the family to this cursed fate. Nathaniel had felt the weight of the curse descend on him, felt the cold grip of the house tightening around his throat. There had been no escape, no way out.

The noose had been waiting for him.

And now, as Anastacia fled from the attic, the same darkness that had taken Nathaniel was coming for her.

Chapter 8

The Cursed Veil

The hidden room was exactly where Nathaniel had said it would be—a concealed passage behind the wall of the mansion's east wing, buried beneath decades of dust and darkness. Anastacia stood before the narrow door, her breath shallow as her fingers traced the edges of the old brass handle. The air was thick with the scent of mildew and decay, the odor of a past that had been deliberately forgotten, left to rot in the shadows. She could almost feel the weight of the generations pressing down on her, suffocating her with secrets long buried.

Nathaniel's voice echoed in her mind. His last words had been haunted, filled with a terror that Anastacia had dismissed at the time, but now clung to her with chilling clarity. "You have to see it for yourself. The room where it all began."

The mansion had always been unsettling, but in the days leading up to this moment, it had become something more than just a house. It had grown alive, as if feeding off the mounting tension, the rising fear in her heart. The walls whispered, the shadows seemed to shift with a life of their own, and the oppressive weight of the family curse hung in the air like a dark cloud.

With trembling hands, Anastacia reached for the brass handle. The metal was cold beneath her fingers, sending a shiver up her spine. She knew that whatever lay beyond this door would change everything. Once she opened it, there would be no going back. The truths she had buried, the secrets she had ignored—everything would be laid bare.

Taking a deep breath, she turned the handle and pushed the door open.

The room beyond was suffocatingly small, no more than ten feet across, and lined with dusty shelves filled with strange and sinister relics. Old books with cracked spines, jars filled with unknown substances, and ancient trinkets that seemed to hum with an energy she couldn't explain. A single window, long neglected and covered in grime, allowed only a sliver of moonlight to filter in, casting long, eerie shadows that danced across the floor like specters of the past.

At the center of the room was a large, ornately carved chest, its surface marred by age, but still imposing in its craftsmanship. The chest was covered in a thick layer of dust, its hinges rusted with the passage of time. It called to her, as if it held the answers to every question, the key to every mystery that had haunted her since the day she set foot in this cursed mansion.

Anastacia approached it cautiously, her heart pounding in her chest, her pulse loud in her ears. The air felt thicker the closer she got, as though the room itself was holding its breath, waiting for her to open the chest and uncover what had been hidden for so long.

She knelt before the chest, her fingers trembling as they brushed against the latch. The metal was brittle and cold, and it gave way with a reluctant creak, as if it hadn't been opened in decades. The silence in the room was deafening, and she could hear nothing but the frantic beating of her heart.

With one final breath, Anastacia lifted the lid.

The chest opened with a groan, releasing a cloud of dust into the stale air. Inside was a collection of old papers, bound together with brittle, yellowed string. They looked ancient, their edges frayed and worn from time. But there was something else in the chest, something beneath the papers that caught the moonlight—a small, ornate dagger, its blade gleaming despite the years of neglect.

Her breath caught in her throat as she reached for the papers, pulling them out carefully. They were fragile, the pages crumbling slightly at the edges as she unwrapped the string. Her eyes skimmed the text, the words blurring together in her panic and disbelief. The handwriting was old, nearly illegible in places, but it was unmistakable.

These were family records.

Not just records—manuscripts. Spells, rituals, and accounts of dark, forbidden practices.

The Glenoire family's hidden legacy.

Her hands shook as she unfolded the pages, her heart pounding in her chest as she began to read. The manuscripts were filled with strange symbols and arcane incantations, rituals that promised wealth and power in exchange for something far darker—something she couldn't yet fully comprehend.

The further she read, the more her mind reeled. The words on the page were not mere superstition or folklore. These were detailed instructions for rituals—rituals that had been performed by her ancestors, right here in this mansion. The spells were designed to bind spirits, summon entities, and extend life at a terrible cost. Blood had been spilled in these very rooms, sacrifices made in secret to maintain the Glenoire family's wealth and status.

The more she read, the clearer it became: the family's fortune had been built on these dark practices, and the mansion itself had been the epicenter of it all. It was not just a home—it was a vessel for something ancient, something that had been feeding off the Glenoire's for generations. The curse wasn't just a story. It was real, and it had been passed down through the bloodline, binding every member of the family to the mansion's will.

This is where it all began, she realized. This is where the family damned itself.

Anastacia felt a surge of nausea as she flipped through the pages, her eyes widening in horror. The manuscripts detailed specific rituals performed by her ancestors—rituals involving blood sacrifices, binding pacts with otherworldly entities, and incantations that tied their souls to the mansion. One passage, in particular, caught her attention, written in a shaky hand and signed by Eleanor Glenoire, her great-grandmother:

"The house knows. It sees everything. We are bound to it now. The ritual cannot be undone, not without great cost. The house will demand more. It always does."

Her stomach churned as she read the final lines of the entry: "One day, the debt will come due. And when it does, there will be no escape. The house will claim us all."

Anastacia's breath came in short, panicked gasps as she let the manuscript fall from her hands, the pages scattering across the floor like dead leaves. Her great-grandmother had known. They had all known. And yet, they had continued the rituals, continued the sacrifices, all to maintain their power and wealth. The house was alive—feeding on them, on their blood, their souls—and now it was her turn.

The air in the room grew colder, and the flickering moonlight seemed to dim, casting deeper shadows across the shelves. Anastacia's gaze drifted to the far corner of the room, where an old mirror stood propped up against the wall. The glass was cracked and stained, but her reflection was still visible, distorted by the fractures.

She stood slowly, her legs weak beneath her, and moved toward the mirror, drawn to it by a force she couldn't explain. Her reflection stared back at her, but there was something wrong. Something in the way her eyes looked—emptier, darker. She swallowed hard, her pulse quickening as she reached out toward the glass, her fingers hovering just above the surface.

In the reflection, something moved behind her.

Anastacia froze, her breath catching in her throat as she turned sharply, her heart pounding in her chest. The room was empty. There was no one there.

But she had seen something. She was sure of it.

Her hands shook as she backed away from the mirror, her mind racing. The manuscripts had detailed rituals designed to bind spirits, to summon forces from beyond. Had her ancestors unleashed something in this house? Had they bound themselves—and their descendants—to a power they couldn't control?

As she stood there, trembling in the cold, dark room, she realized that the house was alive. It had been waiting for her, for this moment. The walls felt like they were breathing, the air thick with the weight of centuries of secrets and lies. The house was hungry, and it was feeding on her fear.

The ground beneath her feet seemed to shift, and she stumbled backward, her hands grabbing for support. The room felt as though it was spinning, the shadows growing darker, more oppressive. She could hear whispers—faint and distant at first, but growing louder with each passing second. They came from the walls, from the very structure of the house itself.

"It's coming."

"You cannot escape."

"The house will take what it is owed."

Anastacia's pulse raced as she turned and fled from the hidden room, her footsteps echoing through the narrow passage as she ran. The walls seemed to close in around her, the air growing heavier with every step. She could feel the mansion watching her, its presence like a dark, suffocating cloud pressing down on her.

Anastacia found herself back in the mansion's grand library, her hands shaking as she rifled through the old books and records that lined the shelves. She had to know more—she had to understand the full extent of the curse, of what her ancestors had done to bind themselves to this monstrous place.

The library had always been her sanctuary, a place of calm and control. But tonight, it felt different. The air was colder here, the shadows deeper, and the books themselves seemed to hum with an energy she had never noticed before.

She pulled a dusty volume from one of the shelves, its spine cracked and worn from age. The book was filled with old accounts of the Glenoire family's history—stories that had been passed down through generations. But these weren't the sanitized versions she had been told as a child. These were darker, filled with tales of strange happenings, unexplained deaths, and whispered rumors of occult practices.

Flipping through the pages, Anastacia's eyes widened as she came across an entry detailing a series of rituals performed by her great-grandfather, Abram Glenoire. According to the account, Abram had been deeply involved in the occult, seeking to extend his life and amass even greater wealth through the use of forbidden magic. He had performed rituals deep within the mansion, rituals that had required blood sacrifices—sacrifices that had bound the spirits of the dead to the house, creating a link between the Glenoire bloodline and the mansion itself.

The rituals had been passed down through the generations, each member of the family contributing to the dark legacy that had ensnared them all. Abram had written extensively about his attempts to control the spirits, to bend them to his will. But as the years went on, his writings became more frantic, more desperate. It was clear that he had lost control, that the spirits he had summoned were no longer under his command.

One passage, in particular, sent chills down Anastacia's spine:

"The house grows stronger with each passing year. It feeds on us, on our fear, on our blood. We thought we could control it, but we were wrong. It controls us. We are bound to it now, forever."

The more she read, the more the truth became clear: the mansion wasn't just a home. It was a prison, a living entity that had been feeding on the Glenoire family for generations. The rituals performed by her ancestors had bound their souls to the house, ensuring that their fates were forever tied to its dark power.

As Anastacia poured over the books and manuscripts, strange occurrences began happening throughout the mansion. The walls groaned and creaked, the sound like the settling of bones. Doors that had been closed swung open of their own accord, the hinges squealing in protest. The temperature in the library plummeted, and she could see her breath in the cold air.

The lights flickered, casting the room into brief moments of darkness, and every time the lights came back on, the shadows seemed to shift, as if they were alive, moving on their own.

And then there were the voices.

They were faint at first, like a soft murmur in the background, but they grew louder as the night went on. They whispered her name, called to her from the darkness, beckoning her deeper into the heart of the mansion.

"Anastacia… Come to us…"

Her heart pounded in her chest as she stood in the center of the library, her eyes darting around the room. The air felt thick, suffocating, as if the mansion itself was pressing down on her, closing in on her from all sides.

She couldn't stay here any longer. She had to get out.

But as she turned to leave, the door to the library slammed shut with a deafening crash, trapping her inside.

The walls seemed to pulse with a dark energy, and the whispers grew louder, more insistent.

"You cannot escape. You are ours now."

Anastacia's pulse raced as she backed away from the door, her eyes wide with terror. The mansion was alive—she could feel it in every creak, every groan of the walls. It was watching her, waiting for her to make her next move.

And she knew, with a sinking feeling of dread, that there was no escape.

Chapter 9

The Author's Final Stroke

The night air in the mansion was suffocating, thick with the residue of everything that had led to this moment. Outside, the storm had finally subsided, the wind and rain no longer lashing against the ancient walls. But inside, the storm raged on. It was as if the very air in the mansion was alive, pulsing with malevolence and anticipation, like a predator waiting for its prey to make one final, fatal mistake.

Anastacia stood in the grand ballroom, her body trembling. Her breath came in shallow gasps, her chest tightening with a fear she hadn't felt before. She had been in control once— of her life, her career, her fate. Now, that illusion had crumbled around her, the weight of the truth pressing down with an unbearable force.

The chandeliers above swayed gently, the light they cast flickering erratically, casting long, wavering shadows across the floor. The mirrors lining the walls reflected distorted versions of her, grotesque and twisted, mocking her in every glance. Each reflection was a reminder of the chaos that had consumed her life, of the darkness that had slowly seeped into every corner of her reality.

She was alone.

Or at least she thought she was.

The mansion was never truly empty. Its presence was everywhere, watching her, waiting. It had been waiting for years, for generations, for this moment. The game was not over yet—it had only just begun.

Her mind raced, her thoughts clouded by the creeping sense of doom that seemed to pervade the very air. She felt eyes on her, the weight of them like a physical presence pressing down on her skin. She knew he was here. The Stranger, the figure that had followed her for days, lurking in the shadows, whispering in her ear when she was most vulnerable.

"This is your story, Anastacia. But you are not the author."

The words echoed in her mind, chilling her to the bone. She had heard them countless times now, but each repetition cut deeper, carving away at the carefully constructed façade she had built around herself. She had always been the one in control—she had written the narrative of her life, shaped her destiny with her own hands. But now, those hands trembled, and she wasn't so sure anymore.

Her gaze swept the room, flitting from one dark corner to the next, searching for any sign of movement. The Stranger had been following her, always just out of sight, lurking in the periphery of her vision. He was there—somewhere. Watching. Waiting. But the mansion seemed to warp and twist around her, making it impossible to tell where he might be hiding.

The grand ballroom seemed to stretch and contract as if the very fabric of reality was bending around her. The chandeliers flickered again, and for a brief moment, the room appeared different—larger, the ceilings impossibly high, the walls shifting in and out of focus. It was as if the mansion was playing tricks on her, bending time and space to its will.

The mansion is alive.

Anastacia's heart pounded in her chest as the thought gripped her. She could feel it now, the pulse of the mansion, the way it seemed to breathe, the way the walls pressed in around her, whispering secrets in a language she couldn't understand. The mansion had been feeding on her, on her family, for generations. It was not just a house—it was a living entity, tied to the curse that had plagued the Glenoire family for centuries.

She wasn't in control. She never had been.

Her gaze drifted to the large, ornate mirror at the far end of the room, the one that Isabelle had insisted she keep. It was draped in a heavy black cloth, as though the mirror itself was too dangerous to be left exposed. Isabelle had spoken of its "special properties," hinting at powers that Anastacia had never cared to understand. She had always avoided the mirror, uncomfortable with the way it seemed to reflect more than just her physical appearance—something deeper, something darker.

But now, she felt drawn to it.

With slow, deliberate steps, Anastacia crossed the room, her heart hammering in her chest. Each step felt like walking through molasses, the air thick and resistant, as if the mansion itself didn't want her to reach the mirror. But she had to see it. She had to face whatever truth the mirror held. Her fingers brushed the edge of the black cloth, and for a moment, she hesitated. She could feel the power emanating from the mirror, a dark, pulsing energy that made her skin crawl. But she couldn't stop now. Not when she was so close. In one swift motion, she yanked the cloth away.

The mirror gleamed in the dim light, its surface smooth and polished. Anastacia stared at her reflection, her breath catching in her throat. Her face was pale, gaunt, her eyes wide with fear. But as she looked closer, she saw something else—something lurking in the shadows behind her.

The Stranger.

Her pulse quickened, her breath coming in short, ragged gasps. She turned quickly, expecting to see him standing behind her. But the room was empty. The grand ballroom stretched out before her, silent and still. There was no one there.

And yet, the feeling of being watched remained. It pressed down on her, a suffocating weight that made it hard to breathe.

She turned back to the mirror, her reflection staring back at her with wide, haunted eyes. But the Stranger was still there, standing just behind her, his presence undeniable. He was real. He had always been real.

"You can't run from this," his voice whispered, low and menacing. "You can't run from the truth."

Anastacia's heart raced, her mind spinning. The truth. What was the truth? The mansion, the curse, the Stranger—they were all part of something larger, something she hadn't yet fully grasped. But as she stood there, staring at the figure in the mirror, the pieces began to fall into place.

The Stranger wasn't just a figment of her imagination. He was tied to the mansion, tied to the curse that had bound her family for generations. He was part of the story—a story that had been written long before she had ever set foot in this house.

And now, the story was reaching its final act.

Anastacia stumbled backward, her vision blurring with fear and confusion. The walls of the ballroom seemed to close in around her, the air thick with tension. The chandeliers above swayed violently, casting erratic shadows across the room, and the mirrors on the walls warped and twisted, reflecting versions of herself that didn't make sense—versions that were younger, older, sometimes even unrecognizable.

Time itself seemed to shift, bending and looping in ways that made her dizzy. One moment, she was standing in the center of the ballroom, the next, she was at the far end of the room, standing before the mirror again. She blinked, trying to make sense of what was happening, but the more she tried to focus, the more the world around her spiraled out of control.

The mirror cracked.

The sound was deafening, like a gunshot, echoing through the empty ballroom. The glass splintered, spider-webbing across the surface, distorting her reflection until it was unrecognizable. The Stranger disappeared, his image vanishing with the cracks, but the damage was done.

The cracks remained.

Anastacia's breath came in ragged gasps, her pulse pounding in her ears. The room around her seemed to close in, the air thick with tension. She had to leave. She had to get out.

But as she turned to flee, the voice returned, louder this time, more insistent.

"This is your story, Anastacia. But you are not the author."

The words echoed in her mind, each one a dagger, cutting deep into the very fabric of her reality. She wasn't the author. She never had been. The mansion, the curse, the Stranger—they were all part of a story that had been written long before she had ever come here. And now, the story was coming to an end.

She stumbled backward, her vision blurring as the room seemed to warp and twist around her. The walls shifted, the floor tilted beneath her feet, and the chandeliers flickered wildly, casting shadows that danced like dark figures in the corners of her vision.

Time looped again.

One moment, she was running toward the ballroom doors, the next, she was standing in front of the mirror once more, her reflection staring back at her with wide, terrified eyes. The cracks in the mirror grew deeper, spreading like a spider's web across the surface, distorting her image beyond recognition.

She wasn't in control. She never had been.

The mansion had always been strange, always unsettling. But now, it felt alive. It breathed, it moved, it twisted and bent time and space to its will. Anastacia could feel it now more than ever. The walls seemed to hum with a low, rhythmic pulse, like the heartbeat of some ancient, malevolent entity. The floors creaked beneath her feet, but the sound wasn't random—it was purposeful, like the mansion was guiding her, pushing her toward some inevitable conclusion.

She had read the manuscripts, had uncovered the dark rituals that her ancestors had performed within these very walls. They had made pacts with forces they didn't understand, bound their souls to the house in exchange for wealth, power, and immortality. But the price had been steep. The mansion had taken something from each of them, piece by piece, until they were little more than hollow shells, consumed by the very darkness they had sought to control.

And now, it was Anastacia's turn.

The mansion had been waiting for her, for this moment. It had been feeding off her fear, her desperation, her unraveling sense of control. The curse was not just some abstract concept—it was a living, breathing force, tied to the mansion, tied to her family, and now, tied to her.

The walls whispered to her, their voices soft and insistent, telling her things she didn't want to hear, things she couldn't ignore.

"You cannot escape."

"You are part of this now."

"The house owns you."

Anastacia stumbled through the twisting hallways, her heart pounding in her chest as the mansion seemed to close in around her. The doors she had once passed through with ease were now locked, the windows sealed shut. The house was trapping her, pulling her deeper into its embrace.

She could feel its presence now, a dark, suffocating force pressing down on her from all sides. It had been manipulating events, controlling the narrative of her life, bending her to its will. The things she had thought were her choices—moving into the mansion, taking over the family legacy, even writing her novels—had all been part of the mansion's plan. She had never been in control. She had been a puppet, dancing on strings she couldn't see.

As she moved deeper into the mansion, the strange occurrences only intensified. Objects that had once been in one room appeared in another, as though the mansion was shifting its contents at will. Portraits on the walls seemed to move, their eyes following her as she passed. Doors that had been open slammed shut behind her, and when she tried to retrace her steps, the hallways twisted and turned, leading her in circles.

Time itself seemed to bend and loop, trapping her in a surreal nightmare. One moment, she would be running through the ballroom, the next, she would find herself back in the hidden room, staring at the manuscripts and the cursed artifacts that had damned her family.

It was as if the mansion was alive, feeding off her fear and confusion, growing stronger with each passing moment.

As Anastacia descended deeper into the heart of the mansion, she wasn't alone. Other figures began to emerge from the shadows—figures she recognized. Marcus, Isabelle, and even Nathaniel appeared before her, their faces twisted with desperation and fear. They had all been caught in the web of the mansion's curse, each of them vying for control, for survival, as the house closed in around them.

"Anastacia!" Marcus called out, his voice echoing through the twisting hallways. He looked frantic, his usually calm demeanor shattered by the terror that gripped him. "We have to get out of here! The house is closing in on us. It's going to take us all!"

Anastacia turned to face him, her breath ragged, her mind spinning. "There is no escape," she whispered, her voice barely audible. "The house owns us."

Isabelle appeared beside them, her eyes wide with fear. "We have to fight it," she said, her voice shaking. "We can't let it win. There has to be a way to break the curse."

But Anastacia knew better. The curse couldn't be broken. It was part of the mansion, part of them. They were all trapped, bound to the house by the dark rituals that had been performed generations ago.

Nathaniel stepped forward, his face pale and haunted. "We're running out of time," he said, his voice hollow. "The mansion… it's alive. It's feeding off us. We can't escape."

The tension in the room was palpable as the four of them stood together, each of them realizing the same terrible truth: there was no way out. The mansion had claimed them all, and now it was playing its final hand.

But even as the walls closed in, even as the air grew thick with the weight of the curse, Anastacia felt a surge of determination. She had been a puppet for too long, controlled by forces she didn't understand. But she wasn't ready to surrender. Not yet.

"This is my story," she said, her voice rising with a newfound strength. "I may not be the author, but I can still write the ending."

The others looked at her, their eyes filled with uncertainty and fear. But they had no choice. The mansion was closing in on them, and if they didn't act now, it would consume them all.

Together, they made their way toward the heart of the mansion, where the final confrontation awaited. The house had been controlling them for too long, bending their lives to its will. But now, they were going to take it back.

Or die trying.

As they reached the mansion's inner sanctum, the air grew impossibly heavy, thick with a dark energy that made it hard to breathe. The walls pulsed with a life of their own, and the whispers grew louder, more insistent, as if the house itself was taunting them, daring them to defy it.

The showdown had begun.

The room they entered was unlike any other in the mansion. It was vast and dark, the walls lined with arcane symbols and strange artifacts that seemed to glow with a faint, otherworldly light. At the center of the room was an altar, ancient and worn, its surface stained with the blood of the countless rituals that had been performed there.

"This is where it ends," Anastacia said, her voice steady despite the fear gnawing at the edges of her mind. "We either take control, or we become part of the house forever."

Marcus, Isabelle, and Nathaniel stood beside her, their faces pale but determined. The air around them seemed to hum with energy, the mansion's presence looming over them like a dark cloud, waiting for them to make their move.

Anastacia stepped forward, her hand reaching for the ancient dagger that lay on the altar. The manuscripts had spoken of a final ritual, a way to sever the ties between the family and the mansion. But it required a sacrifice—a final act of defiance that would either break the curse or bind them to the house for all eternity.

She held the dagger in her hands, her heart pounding in her chest. The others watched her, their eyes filled with fear and hope, waiting for her to make the final decision.

"This is our only chance," she said, her voice steady. "We either fight the house, or we let it consume us."

With a deep breath, Anastacia raised the dagger, preparing to plunge it into the altar, to perform the final act that would either save them or doom them all.

But as she brought the blade down, the room exploded with light, and the mansion roared with fury, its walls shaking violently as it fought to maintain control.

The final battle had begun.

In the end, it was not about who held the power, but about who was willing to sacrifice everything to break free. Anastacia, Marcus, Isabelle, and Nathaniel stood united against the living force of the mansion, their lives and souls hanging in the balance as the house fought to keep them trapped within its cursed walls.

But for the first time in centuries, the mansion faced resistance. And as the final stroke was made, as the dagger pierced the heart of the altar, the house let out a deafening, otherworldly scream.

The mansion began to collapse, its walls crumbling around them, its power fading as the curse was finally broken.

Anastacia, battered and bloodied but alive, stood in the center of the wreckage, the weight of the curse finally lifted from her shoulders.

This had been her story.

And she had written the ending.

Chapter 10

The Silent Reckoning

The world outside the mansion seemed indifferent, as if the horrors that had unfolded within its walls had never happened. The sky was a washed-out gray, and the barren trees stood like skeletal sentinels, stripped of their leaves, swaying faintly in the wind. The storm that had once raged with ferocious fury had long since passed, leaving behind an unnerving stillness. But inside the mansion, time had ceased to flow in a linear way. It had become stagnant, distorted, and suffocating, as if the very fabric of reality was unraveling.

Anastacia sat in the study, her body slumped in the large leather chair. Her eyes were vacant, staring out at the bleak horizon, but seeing nothing. Her hair, once immaculate, now hung in loose, tangled waves around her pale face. Her skin had taken on a ghostly translucence, almost as if she were already fading into the very walls of the mansion. She had become a shadow of herself—a hollow shell trapped in the prison of her own making.

The mansion had won. It had consumed her, just as it had consumed everyone else who had dared to live within its cursed walls.

The memories of the past few weeks played out in her mind on an endless loop: Henry's lifeless body, blood smeared across the floor; Nathaniel's desperate, haunted eyes as he tried to warn her; Marcus's final, chilling words before he had vanished into the dark; and the Stranger, always watching from the shadows. His voice echoed in her mind even now, the same words over and over, like a chant, driving her toward madness:

"This is your story, Anastacia. But you are not the author."

She no longer resisted the truth. She no longer fought the reality of her situation. She had accepted it, just as she had accepted the inevitable end that awaited her. The mansion had been writing her story from the beginning, guiding her toward her own destruction. She had never been in control.

Her fingers absently traced the edge of the desk, the wood cool and smooth beneath her touch. The study, once a place of solace and power, now felt like a tomb. The air was thick with the scent of decay and dust. The windows were streaked with grime, and the heavy curtains hung limp, as though the very soul of the house had been drained.

She glanced at the pile of papers on the desk—the manuscript she had written all those years ago. The story that had foretold everything that was happening to her now. She skimmed the first few lines, but the words blurred together, their meaning lost. It no longer mattered. None of it mattered.

A soft knock at the door broke the oppressive silence. The sound was like a jolt to her numb senses, and for a moment, she didn't respond. But she knew who it was. Detective Lawson had been coming by regularly since Henry's death, always with the same questions, always leaving with the same unanswered suspicions.

The door creaked open, and Lawson stepped into the room, his trench coat buttoned up tightly against the cold. His presence was an intrusion into the suffocating desolation that filled the mansion. He cast a long shadow in the dim light, his eyes sharp as ever as he fixed them on Anastacia.

"Ms. Graves," he said, his voice quiet but firm. "I need to talk to you about Nathaniel."

The mention of Nathaniel's name brought a flicker of life to Anastacia's vacant eyes—something that had been buried beneath layers of denial and numbness. She blinked slowly, her gaze shifting from the window to the detective.

"Nathaniel is dead," she said flatly, her voice hoarse from disuse.

Lawson stepped further into the room, his boots making soft thuds on the hardwood floor. "I know. But I need to understand what happened. I need you to tell me everything."

A bitter smile tugged at Anastacia's lips, but it was hollow, devoid of any real emotion. "What's the point? You already know what happened."

Lawson's eyes narrowed slightly. "I know that something happened, yes. But I don't know why. Or how."

Anastacia turned her gaze back to the window, her hands folding in her lap. "The mansion did it."

Lawson remained silent for a moment, studying her. She could feel his skepticism, his need for rational answers pressing against the fragile remnants of her sanity.

"You're saying the house killed him?" Lawson asked, his voice calm, measured.

Anastacia's eyes fluttered shut for a brief moment as the memories clawed their way to the surface—memories she had tried so hard to lock away. "Not just the house. The curse. The family's curse."

Lawson sighed softly, running a hand through his damp hair. "Ms. Graves, I've heard a lot of stories in my time, but I need you to be straight with me. What exactly happened here?"

Anastacia opened her eyes, her gaze distant as she stared out at the gray sky. "You won't believe me. No one will. But that doesn't change the truth."

Lawson stepped closer, his tone softening. "Try me."

She hesitated, her fingers tracing the smooth surface of the desk. Her mind raced, struggling to find the words to explain something that defied explanation. She had never believed in the supernatural. She had always relied on logic, on control. But the mansion had stripped that away from her, piece by piece, until all that remained was the raw, undeniable truth she had fought so hard to suppress.

"The mansion," she began, her voice barely above a whisper, "it's alive. It's always been alive. My family... we've been tied to it for generations. The curse... it runs through our blood. I didn't want to believe it, but Nathaniel was right. He tried to warn me."

Lawson said nothing, his expression unreadable as he listened.

"It started slowly," Anastacia continued, her voice growing steadier as she spoke. "Little things. Shadows, noises, strange occurrences. I thought it was my imagination, but then Henry died. The note—'Liar.' That was the mansion. It was a warning."

"A warning for what?" Lawson asked, his voice gentle but probing.

"For what was coming," Anastacia replied, her hands curling into fists in her lap. "For Nathaniel's death. For everything."

Lawson crossed his arms, his brow furrowing. "What happened to Nathaniel?"

Anastacia's breath hitched as the memories flooded back, memories of that fateful night when Nathaniel had vanished—taken by the mansion. She had tried to block it out, but now, faced with the detective's questions, she couldn't hide from the truth any longer.

Nathaniel's Fate—The Final Night

It had been two weeks after Henry's death. The mansion had grown darker, more oppressive, with each passing day. The air had been thick with tension, as though the house itself was closing in on them. Nathaniel had become increasingly paranoid, convinced that the curse was coming for him next.

"I have to leave," Nathaniel had told her that night, his eyes wild with fear. He had been pacing the study, his hands shaking as he packed his suitcase. "I have to get out before it's too late."

Anastacia had stood in the doorway, watching him with a mixture of pity and dread. "You can't escape it," she had whispered, her voice barely audible. "The curse... it won't let you go."

Nathaniel had paused, his eyes locking onto hers. There had been desperation in his gaze, a deep, gnawing fear that she hadn't fully understood at the time. "I have to try," he had said, his voice trembling.

And then he had left.

Anastacia had watched from the grand foyer as Nathaniel's car disappeared down the long, winding drive, swallowed by the darkness of the night. The wind had howled through the trees, and the mansion had creaked and groaned, as though in protest. Hours passed, and Nathaniel never returned.

The next morning, his car had been found abandoned at the edge of the property, the doors open, the engine still running. But Nathaniel was nowhere to be found. The police had searched the grounds, combing through the woods and fields, but there was no trace of him. It was as if he had vanished into thin air.

But Anastacia knew the truth.

Nathaniel hadn't left. The mansion had taken him.

Anastacia's voice cracked as she recounted the events to Lawson, her hands trembling in her lap. "He never left the property. The house... it took him."

Lawson's frown deepened, his skepticism clear. "Ms. Graves, with all due respect, houses don't just take people. Are you sure you're remembering this correctly?"

Anastacia's eyes snapped to his, a spark of anger flaring in her chest. "I know what I saw, Detective. I know what happened."

Lawson remained silent, his eyes searching hers for any sign of deceit or delusion. But Anastacia was done pretending. She was done trying to convince herself that everything could be explained away by logic and reason. The truth was simple, and it was horrifying.

The mansion was alive.

And it wanted her next.

"I'm telling you," she said, her voice firm. "The mansion is cursed. It's been cursed for generations. And it won't stop until it's taken everything."

Lawson's lips pressed into a thin line as he considered her words. For a long moment, neither of them spoke, the weight of the conversation hanging heavy in the air.

Finally, Lawson sighed, rubbing the back of his neck. "Look, I don't know what's going on here, but I promise you, we're going to find Nathaniel. We'll keep searching."

Anastacia didn't respond. She knew the search was pointless. Nathaniel was gone. The mansion had claimed him, just as it had claimed Henry, and just as it would claim her. She was next. She could feel it.

Lawson turned to leave, but before he could step out of the room, he paused, glancing over his shoulder. "Ms. Graves," he said quietly. "If there's anything else—anything at all—you need to tell me, now's the time."

Anastacia stared at him, her heart heavy with the weight of the truth she had been trying to deny for so long. But there was nothing left to say. The mansion had already written the final chapter of her story.

And she wasn't the author.

Without another word, Lawson left, the door clicking shut behind him.

Anastacia remained in the study, her gaze drifting back to the window. The sky outside was still gray, the clouds heavy with the promise of rain. But the storm was inside her now, swirling with a force she could no longer control.

The mansion was silent, but she could feel it watching her, waiting for her to make her next move.

The game wasn't over.

Not yet.

The hours passed slowly, the heavy silence of the mansion broken only by the occasional creak of the old floorboards and the soft sigh of the wind outside. Anastacia remained in the study, her mind racing as she replayed Nathaniel's final moments over and over again. He had tried to escape, but the house had taken him. It had swallowed him whole, just as it had done to the others.

But as the night wore on, something inside Anastacia began to shift. She had accepted her fate, resigned herself to becoming another victim of the curse. But now, a flicker of defiance sparked within her. She couldn't let the house win. Not like this. Not without a fight.

For the first time in weeks, Anastacia stood from the chair, her legs unsteady beneath her. She glanced around the study, her gaze landing on the scattered pages of her manuscript. The words that had once foretold her doom now seemed distant, irrelevant. She was still the protagonist of her story, wasn't she? Could she still rewrite the ending?

She moved quickly, her body trembling with the sudden surge of energy. There had to be a way out. There had to be something she had missed. The curse couldn't be unbreakable. Her ancestors had made deals with dark forces, but they had also left clues—clues that she had overlooked.

Anastacia made her way to the grand staircase, her footsteps echoing through the empty halls. The mansion loomed around her, its walls heavy with the weight of centuries of secrets. The air was thick with tension, as if the house was holding its breath, waiting for her to act.

She descended the stairs, her heart pounding in her chest. The house was alive, but so was she. She could feel its presence all around her, pressing in on her, but she refused to be afraid. Not anymore. If Nathaniel had failed, then she would succeed. She had to.

Anastacia found herself standing in the foyer, the massive front doors looming before her. They had always been closed, locked tight as though the house itself had barred her escape. But now, with renewed determination, she reached for the handle. Her hand hovered there for a moment, trembling as the weight of her decision pressed down on her. She could feel the house watching her, waiting to see what she would do.

"You cannot leave," the familiar voice whispered in her mind. "This is your story, Anastacia. But you are not the author."

She clenched her jaw, her fingers tightening around the door handle. "I don't care," she whispered through gritted teeth. "I'm ending this. I'm ending you."

With a sudden burst of strength, Anastacia yanked the door open. The cold night air rushed in, filling her lungs with its crispness. For a moment, she stood there, staring out into the darkness, her breath coming in short gasps. She had done it. She had opened the door.

But before she could take a step, the house fought back.

The floor beneath her feet shifted, the walls groaning as if the entire mansion was coming to life. The door slammed shut with a deafening crash, the sound reverberating through the halls like the roar of a wounded beast. The air grew thick, the temperature plummeting as the house asserted its control.

"You cannot leave," the voice hissed, louder now, more insistent. "You are mine, Anastacia. You have always been mine."

Anastacia stumbled back, her heart pounding in her chest. The walls around her began to pulse, the shadows deepening, stretching out like dark tendrils, reaching for her. The house was fighting her, pulling her back into its embrace.

But she wasn't ready to give up. Not yet.

With a scream of defiance, Anastacia turned and ran. She sprinted through the twisting halls, her breath coming in ragged gasps as the house shifted around her, warping the very space in which she moved. Doors slammed shut before she could reach them, the walls narrowing, forcing her down narrower and narrower paths.

The mansion's malevolence was palpable now, pressing in on her from all sides. The floor beneath her feet felt unstable, as if it were no longer solid. The house was trying to trap her, to swallow her whole.

But Anastacia kept running.

She didn't know where she was going—there was no clear destination. All she knew was that she couldn't stop. She had to keep moving. She had to stay ahead of whatever force the mansion had unleashed.

As she turned a corner, she found herself back in the grand ballroom. The room was dark, the chandeliers swaying ominously above her. The mirrors that lined the walls were cracked, their surfaces distorted, reflecting grotesque versions of her as she stumbled into the center of the room. The house had brought her here for a reason.

"This is where it ends," the voice whispered in her ear.

Anastacia's breath hitched as the shadows in the room began to coalesce, forming dark, twisted figures that loomed around her. The Stranger was there, his presence palpable, though he remained just out of sight. The walls pulsed with a dark energy, as if the mansion itself was closing in, preparing to deliver the final blow.

But Anastacia wasn't done fighting.

With a roar of defiance, she grabbed the nearest object—a heavy candlestick from the mantle—and swung it wildly at the figures that surrounded her. The shadows dissipated under the force of her blows, but they reformed quickly, as if the house was toying with her, prolonging her suffering.

She fell to her knees, her body trembling from exhaustion, the candlestick clattering to the floor beside her.

The mansion was winning. She could feel it.

But then, in the darkness, she remembered something— something Nathaniel had said before he had vanished.

"The house feeds on our fear," he had whispered to her one night. "If we give in to it, it will consume us. But if we fight... if we don't let it control us..."

Anastacia's eyes widened as the realization hit her. The house was powerful, yes, but it was feeding off her fear, her despair. It had always been feeding off the emotions of those trapped within its walls. If she gave in, if she surrendered, it would win.

But if she fought back...

Anastacia took a deep breath, her pulse slowing as she forced herself to stand. The shadows still loomed around her, the house still groaned with malevolent intent, but she could feel a shift within herself—a quiet resolve that had been buried beneath her fear.

"I'm not afraid of you," she whispered, her voice steady.

The shadows recoiled, as if wounded by her words.

"I'm not afraid," she said again, louder this time. She stepped forward, her gaze locking onto the nearest mirror. The cracks in the glass seemed to shimmer, the distorted reflection staring back at her, but she didn't look away.

The house roared in fury, the walls trembling violently as it tried to reassert control. But Anastacia stood her ground.

"You don't control me," she said, her voice firm, unyielding. "You never did."

And with those words, the mansion began to crumble.

The walls buckled, the ceiling groaning as the house's foundation shook. The dark energy that had surrounded her dissipated, and the shadows that had once loomed so menacingly faded into nothingness.

Anastacia stood in the center of the collapsing mansion, her body trembling but her mind clear.

She had won.

The mansion had crumbled to ruins, its power finally broken. Anastacia stood amidst the wreckage, the cold night air

biting at her skin, but she didn't care. She was free. For the
first time in her life, she was truly free.

The curse had been lifted, the house's hold on her shattered.
And for the first time in years, she could write her own story,
or so she thought.

Epilogue

Shadows Yet to Fall

The mansion was silent.

The storm had passed, leaving behind a world washed in gray. The sky hung low over the cliffs, and the sea below, which had raged with fury only hours before, was now unnervingly calm. There was an eerie tranquility in the aftermath, as though nature itself had paused to consider what had transpired within the mansion's dark, twisted halls. The wind no longer howled through the trees, the rain no longer lashed against the windows. Everything was still—too still.

Inside, the house remained a tomb. Its once grand halls and towering rooms, filled with life and secrets, now sat cold and empty, save for the lingering presence of something ancient and insidious. The mansion had a way of holding onto things—memories, people, souls. And it had claimed many. Anastacia sat in the grand foyer, her hands folded neatly in her lap, her eyes staring blankly ahead. Her mask of control, the one she had worn so meticulously for so long, had cracked and fallen away. The light that had once burned so fiercely in her was gone, extinguished by the very force she had thought she could conquer. The mansion had claimed her, just as it had claimed her ancestors, and just as it had claimed others before them. She had become one with the house—a living relic, trapped by the same walls she had once believed she could control.

She could feel the mansion around her now, its presence no longer subtle or hidden. The house breathed with her, its pulse syncing to her own, its ancient walls vibrating with a life that was as old as the stone itself. It was more than a building; it was a living entity, and it had been waiting for her. She had been a fool to think she could escape its grasp. There was no escape. There never had been.

At her feet, the manuscript lay open, its pages yellowed with age, the ink faded but still legible. She didn't need to read the words again—she knew them by heart. These were her words, her story, written long ago when she had been younger, more ambitious, and filled with the belief that she could bend fate to her will. The story had been her way of imposing order on the chaos around her, of shaping the world to her design. But now, as she gazed at the final lines, she understood the cruel truth.

"This is your story, but you are not the author."

The voice echoed in her mind, a whisper that had tormented her for months, growing louder and more insistent as the mansion's grip on her tightened. At first, she had resisted, fought back against the creeping certainty that she wasn't in control. But in the end, the voice had been right. She had never been the one writing the story. The mansion had been guiding her, pushing her toward this moment, toward her inevitable fall.

The manuscript ended with a single word: FINIS. But Anastacia knew it wasn't the end. The mansion's story would continue, as it always had, waiting for the next soul to step into its trap. It was patient, this house. It would wait, as it had waited for her. The cycle would begin again, and the mansion would claim yet another victim.

Her eyes fluttered shut, and her breath came in shallow, even gasps. The house was quiet now, but she could feel it watching, waiting. It was never truly silent. It would be patient, just as it had been patient with her. It would wait for the right moment, for the next person to step through its doors, unaware of the darkness that lurked within its walls. And when they did, the story would begin again.

In the distance, a soft creak echoed through the house, followed by the sound of footsteps—slow, deliberate, moving toward her. The mansion was not empty, after all.

Anastacia didn't open her eyes. She didn't need to.

The Stranger was here.

And the story would never end.

The storm's fury had passed, but the town remained under a dark cloud. News of what had transpired at the mansion spread like wildfire, carried on the lips of those who dared speak of it. The Glenoire mansion had always been a source of unease, but now, it had become something more. The death at the masquerade, the whispers of strange occurrences inside the mansion, and the sudden silence from those who had attended the event painted a chilling picture that no one wanted to face directly.

As the sun rose over the town, casting long shadows across the cobbled streets, the townspeople gathered in hushed groups. The mansion loomed on the cliffs, silent and foreboding, as it always had. But now, something felt different. Even those who had never believed the old stories couldn't shake the feeling that something had changed. The mansion's influence, once confined to rumor and superstition, had reached out and touched the town in a way that could not be ignored.

Law enforcement had been called in—local officers first, followed by investigators from the city. They approached the mansion with caution, their footsteps hesitant as they ascended the winding path to the iron gates. The gates stood open, as though inviting them in, but there was an air of malevolence that hung over the property. The officers exchanged uneasy glances before stepping inside.

The mansion greeted them with silence. The grand rooms, the long corridors, the vast ballroom—everything was untouched, as if the chaos of the previous night had never happened. But there was a heaviness in the air, a sense that the house itself was watching, waiting.

They found Anastacia in the grand foyer, sitting perfectly still, her hands in her lap, her face pale and expressionless. The investigators tried to speak to her, but she didn't respond. It was as if she had become a part of the mansion itself, as cold and lifeless as the stone walls that surrounded her.

The investigation into Henry's death and the events of the masquerade yielded few answers. The officers combed through the mansion, interviewing the remaining guests, but no one could explain what had happened. The accounts varied—some spoke of objects moving on their own, of doors that led to nowhere, of strange figures appearing in mirrors. Others were too shaken to speak at all.

But one thing was clear: no one could leave. The investigators, like the guests before them, found themselves trapped within the mansion's shifting halls. The exits, once clear and open, had become twisted and confusing, as though the house was determined to keep them inside.

Back in the town, the disappearance of the investigators sent ripples of fear through the community. Those who had once dismissed the stories of the Glenoire mansion as mere superstition began to rethink their skepticism. There were hushed meetings in the town square, discussions of what should be done. Some wanted to send more help, while others believed that the mansion should be left alone—that it had claimed enough lives, and anyone who ventured inside was doomed.

Old-timers like Jonas Tuck, who had seen the mansion's eerie lights as a boy, spoke in grave tones about the power of the house. "It's always been like this," Jonas would say, his voice trembling. "It doesn't matter who owns it or what they think they can do with it. The house decides. It always decides."

The townspeople tried to carry on with their lives, but the presence of the mansion weighed heavily on them. Children were forbidden from going near the cliffs, and even the adults found themselves avoiding the narrow path that led to the estate. Every so often, someone would look up at the mansion and swear they saw a light flickering in one of the windows. But when they looked again, it was gone.

The Fate of Those Left Behind

Inside the mansion, the guests who had survived the masquerade were left to grapple with their own demons. Caroline, Anastacia's assistant, had always prided herself on being composed, on handling any crisis with calm efficiency. But after the events of the masquerade, she could no longer keep up the facade. She had seen things—things she couldn't explain, things she couldn't forget. The mansion had shown her something in the mirrors, something that had shaken her to her core. She tried to leave, but like the others, she found herself wandering the halls, always ending up back where she started.

Michael, the businessman, had once been so confident, so sure of himself. But the mansion had stripped away his bravado, exposing the fragile man beneath. He had seen his reflection in one of the grand mirrors during the masquerade, but it hadn't been him. The man in the mirror had been older, broken, defeated. And as Michael watched, the reflection had smiled—a cruel, knowing smile that promised he would never escape his fate.

Nathaniel, Anastacia's brother, had been unraveling long before the night of the masquerade. But now, he was barely holding on. He wandered the mansion like a ghost, muttering to himself about the family curse, about the house's power.

As the days turned into weeks, the mansion claimed them all. One by one, they faded into the shadows, becoming part of the house's long, twisted history. The town, too afraid to investigate further, eventually stopped asking questions. The mansion, as it always had, was left to its own devices.

Drawn to the Mansion

Months passed. The town settled into a tense quiet, and life returned to something resembling normalcy. But the mansion's influence was far from over.

Evelyn checked into the local inn, asking questions about the mansion, about the events that had taken place there. The townspeople were reluctant to speak, but she had a way of getting information out of people. They told her about Anastacia, about the masquerade, about the strange occurrences that had taken place. They warned her to stay away, but Evelyn's curiosity only grew.

Late one night, Evelyn made her way to the cliffs, the wind howling through the trees as she approached the iron gates. They stood open, as though waiting for her.

She stepped inside.

The mansion loomed before her, its windows dark and empty, its stone walls covered in creeping ivy. But as she stood there, staring up at the towering structure, she felt something stir within her—a pull, a connection. It was as though the mansion had been waiting for her, just as it had waited for Anastacia.

Evelyn took a deep breath and stepped forward.

As she crossed the threshold, the door swung shut behind her with a soft click.

Evelyn entered the room, her presence both quiet and commanding. Anastacia regarded her carefully, sensing the weight of unspoken knowledge behind her calm expression. 'So, you're the one who's been watching,' Anastacia said, her voice measured. 'And you're the one who's been hiding,' Evelyn replied, a small smile tugging at the corner of her lips. Their meeting had been inevitable, two women bound by forces neither fully understood—until now.

The mansion had a new guest.

And the story was far from over

.

FIRST LOOK

Whispers of the Veil

A FATED DECEPTION SAGA

PREQUEL

Before there was power, there was pain.

Before the lies, there was silence.

Before the woman they feared, there was a girl no one protected.

Anastacia Graves wasn't born ruthless—she was shaped that way.

Whispers of the Veil unravels the haunting legacy that created the enigmatic force at the center of *Fifty Shades of Deception*. Long before she inherited the cursed Glenoire mansion, Anastacia learned to survive a different kind of darkness—the kind that hides behind perfect smiles, polished dinner tables, and family portraits.

From an ice-cold mother who weaponized beauty, to a father who turned manipulation into bedtime stories, Anastacia's childhood was a battlefield. Her only ally? Nathaniel, the older brother who did everything he could to shield her from the storm… even when it nearly destroyed him.

But family wasn't the only danger. Friendships twisted into rivalry. Love grew sharp edges. And trust—well, trust was a luxury Anastacia could never afford.

As the years unfold, she battles betrayal from all sides—an affair between her husband and her closest friend, a past lover who won't let go, and the seductive pull of a legacy soaked in secrets. Every chapter pulls back the curtain on the woman behind the mansion—the girl who learned to read danger in silence, to wear control like armor, and to master the art of deception before she ever knew its name.

But beneath the steel and strategy lies a truth even Anastacia doesn't see coming.

Because some veils don't just hide the past…

They protect you from it.

And once they're lifted, nothing will ever be the same.

Excerpt

Whispers of the Veil

She was nine when she learned how to smile through betrayal.

Twelve when she realized silence could be a weapon.

Sixteen when she discovered her body could be armor.

And twenty-seven when she watched the two people she trusted most tear her world apart.

Anastacia stood at the edge of the ballroom, champagne untouched in her hand, eyes fixed on the soft, flirtatious laugh echoing from the terrace. Alexandria's laugh.

Her best friend.

His mistress.

The crystals above her caught the light just right, casting diamond-shaped shadows along the marble floor—flickers of beauty meant to distract from everything rotten underneath.

A familiar voice pulled her back.

"You knew," Marcus said quietly, stepping in behind her.

"Didn't you?"

Anastacia didn't flinch.

"I always know," she whispered.

Then she turned to face him, her expression unreadable. "But knowing and caring those are two very different things."